Praise for Kelly Ja   ⏤n's
Jilted

"Kelly Jamieson...showed us again that she is a gifted storyteller. Her characters are flawed but evolving, the story moves at a decent pace without feeling rushed, solutions are believable, and best of all we know there's more to come in Promise Harbor!"

~ *Guilty Pleasures Book Reviews*

"Kelly Jamieson did a terrific job conveying the all encompassing sexual tension between Josh and Devon, the combustible sparks made my own skin prickle as I bit my nails impatient to finally see them give into their attraction."

~ *Ex Libris*

Jilted

Kelly Jamieson

SAMHAIN
PUBLISHING

Samhain Publishing, Ltd.
11821 Mason Montgomery Road, 4B
Cincinnati, OH 45249
www.samhainpublishing.com

Jilted
Copyright © 2014 by Kelly Jamieson
Print ISBN: 978-1-61921-694-5
Digital ISBN: 978-1-61921-428-6

Editing by Lindsey Faber
Cover by Angela Waters

First Samhain Publishing, Ltd. electronic publication: March 2013
First Samhain Publishing, Ltd. print publication: January 2014

Dedication

To my three lovely author partners in this series, Erin Nicholas, Meg Benjamin and Sydney Somers, and to editor Lindsey Faber—it has been a privilege working with you amazing, talented ladies on this project! Also thanks to the Nine Naughty Novelists who patiently brainstormed titles with us, and to beta reader extraordinaire Kim—you rock!

Prologue

Josh Brewster's head pounded, but he tried to focus on the minister standing at the front of St. Mark's Methodist Church. Allie stood beside him, holding his arm in a death grip, looking pale and shaky.

"You okay?" he whispered, looking down at her. Hell, she'd lost even more weight lately. She looked like she was drowning in that fluffy white dress, and the makeup she'd applied didn't hide how pale her cheeks were or the dark circles beneath her eyes. When he'd watched her walk down the aisle on her father's arm, he'd been...dismayed. Worried. He patted her hand on his forearm.

She swayed yet again and nodded. "Sure. Why not?"

"You look...funny." He closed his eyes briefly. Damn. That wasn't exactly how a groom was supposed to react to seeing his bride on their wedding day. But she really did not look great. She still hadn't gotten over the death of her mom and all the stress of looking after her family. He knew what that was like. Hopefully this wedding would be a new start for everyone.

Mrs. Gurney continued playing the piano, the song that had accompanied Allie and her father down the aisle.

"I worked for two hours this morning to look like this," she whispered back.

The smell of alcohol reached his nose. Was that fumes from his hangover? Or Allie's? Or... "Are you drunk?" he asked with a frown. Was *that* why she looked so awful?

"It's Bernie's fault."

"You're drunk?" he repeated. "Jesus, Allie."

"You're not supposed to say 'Jesus' in church." She frowned. "You're not supposed to say 'Jesus' like *that* in church."

Josh's jaw locked. He couldn't blame her for drinking the night before the wedding. Hell, he'd done the same thing. But the day *of* the wedding...good Christ.

"Josh?" she asked as the song finally came to an end.

"It's okay, Allie," he whispered. "Let's...just do this."

"Dearly beloved, we are gathered here today to unite this man and this woman in holy matrimony."

Then a loud voice at the back of the church said, "Oh, hell no."

Josh's head snapped around. He winced at the stab of pain behind his eyes, and stared at the man striding down the center aisle toward them. The guy wasn't exactly dressed for a wedding, wearing jeans and boots and a faded hoodie. What the hell was going on? Was there some kind of emergency outside the church?

"Gavin?" Allie squeaked.

What the fuck? Gavin? "This is Gavin?" he asked Allie. She was staring wide-eyed at the guy.

What the hell was he doing there? Josh's head throbbed even more as he gave it a shake.

"What do you think you're doing?" Josh demanded, frowning at him. Christ, the guy looked rough—unshaven, wrinkled clothes, bloodshot eyes—

"I'm here to talk to Allie."

Josh kept himself between Gavin and Allie. This lunatic busting into their wedding wasn't laying a hand on her. "We're kind of in the middle of something." *Asshole.*

"Yeah, this can't wait." Gavin looked past Josh to Allie. "I

10

need to talk to you. Now."

Josh glanced at Allie, who was as white as her wedding dress, her eyes round. When Gavin made a move toward her, Josh blocked him. He wanted to punch him but kept his fists at his side. "I don't think so, Gavin."

Gavin sighed and they locked eyes. Josh glared at him. Silence filled the church, and out of the corner of his eye Josh caught the flash of a camera. Fuck, people were taking pictures of this!

"Listen," Gavin said. "I can do this here in front of the whole town. I don't mind. I'm leaving here with Allie one way or another. But I think keeping some of this private might be appropriate." He leaned around Josh to look at Allie. "I have some things I need to say before you say I do to another man, Al."

Now? He wanted to say things to her *now?* After he'd dumped her, disappeared and broken her heart? Josh narrowed his eyes, stepped closer and lowered his voice. "Don't do this, Gavin. Haven't you messed with her enough? Just let her be happy."

"That's exactly what I want to do." Gavin lifted his chin, his mouth tight. "Is that what *you* want?"

Was he fucking *kidding?* "I'm standing next to her in a tux in front of a minister," Josh said incredulously. "What do you think?"

"I think that if you don't let her talk to me, you know that she'll always wonder. You don't want that, do you? To have your wife wondering about another man?"

Josh blew out a long breath and shoved his hand through his hair. Hell. Allie had been crazy in love with Gavin. But they'd broken up over a year ago. She was over him. Wasn't she? She was marrying *him,* for Chrissake. They cared about each other. This wedding was going to turn things around for both their families, and especially for Allie. He half turned to his bride, ready to ask if she wanted him to kick this guy's ass out of there. "Allie?"

But her gaze was focused on Gavin. "What would I wonder?" she asked.

Damn.

"You'd wonder what I had to say to you so badly that I would fly over four thousand miles so I could rush in here to stop your wedding."

Allie stared at Gavin for what seemed like forever. Josh got a sinking feeling in his stomach as he stood there, on the outside, watching them joined in an intense eye lock. Silence filled the church all the way to the high ceiling. Allie looked out at the congregation, then back at Gavin. What was going through her head?

"Allie?" Gavin said again.

She pressed her lips together and shook her head. "You're too late," she whispered.

But Josh caught the glint of tears in her eyes. Aw, hell.

"Bullshit," Gavin said. He stepped forward, bent and hauled her up into his arms, the skirt of her dress trailing to the floor, and headed for the side door.

"Gavin!" She gave a feeble kick.

Josh stepped forward. "Just a damn minute—" he began, adrenaline flashing through his veins as Gavin manhandled Allie.

Gavin turned. "Give me a chance," he said. "Let me talk to her. Let me tell her what I came here to say. Then if she wants to come back, I'll walk her down the aisle myself."

Without waiting for an answer Gavin turned back to the door. He said something to Allie in a low voice, something Josh couldn't hear. Arms linked around his neck, Allie gazed up at him raptly and whispered something back.

Whoa. The look on Allie's face...

Mrs. Gurney sprang to open the door, and Gavin stepped out into the June sunshine with Josh's bride in his arms.

Josh looked at the crowd of stunned faces, and a wave of heat swept over him. Jesus. Was he seriously being left at the altar? Unbelievable! Talk about humiliating.

Then his gaze caught on Devon. His ex-girlfriend, sitting there between Ben Hancock and Hayley Stone, looking just as flabbergasted as everyone else. For a split second, their eyes met and something passed between them, but he dragged his gaze away from her.

Allie had just been abducted by some crazed mountain man. She was fragile and stressed out and...and possibly drunk. He could not let this happen.

He strode to the door to follow them outside.

Chapter One

One month earlier...

The envelope didn't particularly look like something that was going to induce a heart attack.

Rubbing the back of her neck, which was always sore lately, Devon separated it from the rest of her mail, the thick, glossy paper and elegant script standing out from the bills and junk mail. It looked like a wedding invitation. Curious, she ripped it open.

And her heart seized.

For a long, painful moment she stared at it. Josh and Allie were getting married.

Josh and Allie were getting married.

A shaft of pain shot through her, a pain so fierce she almost went to her knees there in the foyer of her Boston apartment. She leaned into the wall for support, her vision darkening around the edges.

Married. Josh and Allie.

She closed her eyes as another wave of pain swept over her.

The man she'd loved with every breath in her body was going to marry her best friend. Well, former best friend. Things had been... Well, there hadn't been much of anything between her and Allie since Devon had learned from Facebook that Josh and Allie were "in a relationship".

Allie had called her not long after that, sounding hesitant and nervous. "I didn't want you to hear from someone else," she'd said.

"Too late." Devon had laughed a little. "I already heard."

"So you're...okay with it? With me and Josh?"

"Of course!" Maybe her voice had been a little too loud, a little too cheery. "Things were over between Josh and me ages ago."

"Well, good. We didn't plan this—it just...happened."

"I'm sure."

The conversation had been short, deliberately cheerful and nonchalant. And then Devon had laid down on her bed and cried.

That had been almost a year ago, and she hadn't talked to Allie since. After torturing herself by stalking Allie and Josh on Facebook, looking for any mention of them together, she'd finally unfriended them for her own good. So this wedding invitation came right out of the blue. Why the hell was Allie sending her an invitation to their wedding?

Devon moved into her apartment, still holding the small card. A glass of wine might be a good idea. No. Make that a bottle. She yanked open her refrigerator and pulled out the nearly full bottle of fine sauvignon blanc. As she sloshed a generous serving into a glass, she looked again at the invitation.

The wedding was a month away, to be held in the town she'd grown up in—Promise Harbor, Massachusetts.

And then Devon started laughing. As if she was going to go back to Promise Harbor for any reason. But for the wedding of her ex-boyfriend and ex-best friend? Ha! Hilarious! She leaned against the counter and laughed, but a chuckle turned to a sob, and she picked up her glass and gulped a big swallow of wine.

Only an hour later, Allie phoned. Devon gripped the phone tightly.

"Hey," Allie said, her voice gentle. "I called to see if you got the invitation."

"I did." Devon pasted on a smile even though Allie couldn't see it, because she knew it would make her sound happier. "Congratulations! I was surprised."

"Um. Yeah. Thanks, Devon. Are you going to come?"

Devon almost snorted and said, *Are you nucking futs?* but Allie spoke again. "I hope you will," she continued. "Josh and I would both love it if you came."

Hearing Josh's name made her heart bump in her chest. "Oh. Really."

"Yes. Really."

"I'm so busy, Allie..." Shit. She didn't have an excuse invented. She'd planned to RSVP her regrets on the impersonal little card included with the invitation, regrets with no explanation necessary. "You know what my job is like..."

"I know, but surely you can take a couple of days off. Your dad would love to see you."

Devon stared at her cell phone in disbelief. "Yeah, I doubt that."

"Well, *we* would. It would mean a lot if you would come. I know it would be hard for you..."

At that, Devon's chin went up and her shoulders straightened. "Why would it be hard?" she asked coolly.

"Because you and Josh...you know..."

"I told you before, Allie, things were done between us a long time ago."

"Oh good." Relief made Allie's voice breathy. "I'm so relieved to hear that. Because, you know, I do feel a little...well, bad, and I'm sorry that...well, we haven't talked in a long time and I had the feeling you were hurt when Josh and I started dating, and I don't want to hurt you, Dev. Really."

Devon's eyes burned and her chest tightened. "I'm not hurt. I'm fine, Allie."

"Are you sure?"

Devon squeezed her eyes shut. She hated that tone in Allie's voice, as if Allie felt sorry for her. She lifted a hand and touched her fingertips to the inner corner of one eye, and they came away wet. But she forced her voice to be steady. "Of course I'm sure. And it wouldn't be hard for me to come to the wedding. Like I said, I'm happy for you both."

"Oh good! It will be so great to see you. You haven't been home for so long."

Devon's eyes widened. Had she agreed to attend the wedding? No, she had not. But somehow Allie thought she was coming, and if she backed out now, Allie would think she was lying about being over Josh and being happy for them.

Which she totally was.

She inhaled a deep breath. "I'll see if I can juggle things at work so that I can come."

"Oh, that would be *so* great."

When the call ended, Devon slumped on her couch in her twentieth-story apartment overlooking downtown Boston, the city now spread like multicolored jewels below her—citrine, topaz and sparkling diamonds. In the distance the spires of the Zakim Bridge stretched into the night sky.

She couldn't do it. She'd find some excuse. Something at work would come up and she just wouldn't be able to get away.

Then she thought of Allie saying how they knew it would be hard for her, and once again she straightened. She did not want them feeling sorry for her. She had a great life. A successful career. A beautiful home. A busy social life. So she had no husband or fiancé or boyfriend even. In fact it had been a few months since she'd even had a date, but that was just because she was so busy and worked such long hours. That was no reason for them to feel sorry for her.

It was true she hadn't been home for a while. The thought

of seeing her dad made her stomach tense a little, and truthfully she'd rather eat her Jimmy Choo pumps than go back to Promise Harbor and be reminded of all the reasons she'd wanted to leave.

The thought of seeing Josh one more time, one last time before he married someone else, pulled at something inside her...but god, could she really bear to see him marry someone else? To marry Allie?

Well, she had a month to figure out some way to get out of it.

The next afternoon, her boss called her in to his office near the end of the day. "I'm afraid I have some bad news," Mel began, a funereal expression on his face. "This isn't going to be easy."

She frowned. What was the problem? Another issue with the Halbert account?

"I'm very sorry to have to tell you this."

She tamped down her impatience and tried to smile encouragingly at him. Her head ached, as it usually did these days, and she resisted the urge to massage her aching neck muscles.

"You know the challenges we've been facing recently," he continued. "The investment banking industry has just gone through one of the toughest period in its history."

She nodded slowly.

"Unfortunately in an economic downturn, when a company is fighting to stay alive, there are few good choices. We've had to make some difficult decisions."

Unease began to squirm inside her. *Would you get to the point...*

"To remain competitive, we're going to have to restructure our organization."

She narrowed her eyes a little at him, her mind working to figure out what he was saying. Somehow she had a feeling this "restructuring" wasn't going to be about a promotion.

"What I'm saying is, we're going to have to reduce the size of our workforce."

"Oh." Oh no. Layoffs were never a good thing.

"I'm sorry, Devon."

Good god, were those tears in his eyes? Her insides tightened and her fingers curled around the armrests of the chair she sat in. He wasn't talking about...her? Was he?

"This decision is no reflection upon you as a person or upon your individual contributions to the firm."

"Me?" Her voice came out dry and rough. She coughed.

"I know that this news comes as a shock to you and that this decision will be difficult to fully understand."

She shook her head. "Um..."

"We'll give you time to gather your belongings and clear out your desk. Or if you prefer, you can leave right now and we'll pack your things up and have them delivered to your home."

Holy snapping duck shit! She shook her head again, still trying to comprehend what was happening. "You're *firing* me?"

"No! Laying you off. It's an economic decision, Devon. As I said, it's no reflection on your work. But you have the least seniority."

"Am I the only one being laid off?"

"No." Once again she thought he was about to cry. "Ten people from this department are losing their jobs."

"Oh. My. God."

"I'm sure this news is quite upsetting to you. Is there

anyone that you would like to call? Can I call someone for you?"

She blinked rapidly at the stinging in the corners of her eyes. Weirdly, the only name that came to mind at that moment was Josh. Not her mom or her dad or a best friend. Steady, dependable, loyal Josh. At that moment, all she could think was how much she wanted his strong arms around her, his broad chest to press her face against.

But that was never going to happen again.

It seemed like it took a couple of hours for her to get control of her emotions enough to speak, but it was probably only a moment. Never let them see you sweat was her motto. She lifted her chin and straightened her shoulders. "No," she said. "I'm fine." She swallowed, her throat still tight and aching. "I'd like to thank you for the opportunity to work here. I've enjoyed it very much." She'd poured her heart and soul and entire frickin' life into this job. "I've learned so much, and I know that will serve me well wherever I end up."

Relief flashed on Mel's round face. He probably expected her to cry or have a tantrum. Or, when she saw the security guard near the door of his office as she left, maybe they'd even expected worse than that. Meep. They should know she was the least likely person to throw a tantrum...or worse.

She packed up her belongings with hands that shook just a little, her insides knotted into a hard ball. It felt unreal, like this couldn't really be happening to her. But it was.

The next morning when she didn't have any reason to get up, it was tempting to just lie in bed and give in to another crying jag. But Jeebus, she couldn't let this happen to her. She had contacts in the business. She'd have a new job by the end of the day. She jumped out of bed and, with a pot of coffee near her laptop and cell phone, started doing research and making calls.

By the end of the day, she didn't have a new job. By the

end of the week, she didn't have a new job. She had a bruised and battered ego and a growing sense of desperation. She kept telling herself a week wasn't very long to be unemployed. They'd given her a small severance package, and yeah, she could collect some unemployment benefits, but she was uncomfortably aware of her miniscule savings. She bit her lip as she looked around the apartment she probably couldn't afford, furnished with lovely things she shouldn't have splurged on. Holy shnikes!

She knew what she had to do. She had to network. Perseverance was the key.

But nearly a month later, she still had no job.

Giving off an air of desperation was a fast way to kill any interest whatsoever, so in one last effort she dressed in her best Donna Karan suit for a lunch she'd arranged with someone with whom she'd gone to college. Martin worked at Heffington International, a boutique investment bank. This was the kind of company that was lowest on her list. She was the girl who'd been recruited on campus by places like Goldman, and Morgan, and the company she'd ended up with, Englun and Seabrook. Clearly, she was ready to take a salary cut. Hell, she was ready to lick someone's boots and work for free. Okay, not really. Well, maybe.

"We are hiring," Martin told her. "We're making money, although we're not really up that much in terms of revenues. But hey, we're not receiving federal bailout monies, and we don't have a big portfolio of toxic assets."

"Tell me more," she murmured, poking her fork into her Cobb salad in the elegant downtown restaurant where she'd lunched many times but which she could no longer afford.

"It's a great company to work for," Martin said. "We've established ourselves as a trusted and respected advisor. We're knowledgeable about specific issues and opportunities affecting companies' strategies, operations, and organic and external

21

growth prospects on a global basis."

"So the company is solid."

"Yeah. Hell yeah."

"Who do I have to talk to there?"

Martin frowned. "The HR director is William Mudge. But you've just missed him. He's just left for three weeks' vacation."

Shnikes! But she kept her expression carefully pleasant. "Three weeks? Oh dear. Isn't someone covering for him while he's away?"

"Nah. He's the one who makes the decisions. In consultation with the partners, of course." He frowned. "I thought I'd heard they'd hired someone a couple of weeks ago and then somehow the offer fell through."

Urgency rose inside her. Cripes, if they were actively hiring and had already made one offer to someone else that hadn't worked out, they were probably ready to make another offer. Maybe they already had offered to someone on their short list. "Damn. I wish I'd talked to you sooner. But I guess it is getting into the summer holiday season." She'd already run into this roadblock a few times.

"Yeah." He grinned. "He's off to Greenbush Island with the family. Oceanside Inn. Nice place."

Greenbush Island? Devon sat up straighter. "Really? I grew up close to there. Promise Harbor."

"Oh yeah? Nice area. Very quaint."

Yeah, that was the word.

"I'm invited to a wedding there this weekend," she said slowly.

Holy shitballs. Her mind started racing as she and Martin talked more about the private equity business focused on leading middle-market, consumer-oriented companies. The company she now had a burning need to work for.

William Mudge. He was going to be on the island only a short ferry ride away from Promise Harbor.

Where she was invited to a wedding.

But, Jeebus Crust, it was Josh and Allie's wedding, the wedding she'd already decided she was *not* going to, and just thinking about it caused a stab of pain in her chest. Could she do it?

Chapter Two

She could do it.

She'd repeated the mantra all the way from Boston to Promise Harbor. Now she was almost there. She gripped the steering wheel as she exited I-93. She was having serious doubts about her ability to pull this off now.

She'd wanted to come back and show everyone she was not a rejected, lonely loser—she was a happy, successful businesswoman who could attend the wedding of her former boyfriend and best friend, because she was over him. But the reality now was—she was unemployed, alone, and only a modest bank account stood between her and having to sublet her apartment and move somewhere cheaper. As for being over Josh... Well, she didn't have much choice about that.

Why had she come?

Oh yeah. William Mudge. Heffington International.

The familiar sign greeted her: *Promise Harbor, Population 20,121. We promise you'll love us.*

She smiled. As a kid she'd always asked how they knew exactly how many people lived there, and did the mayor, Marbell Jacobs, go and change the sign if someone moved away, or every time a baby was born?

She passed the beach—pale, grassy dunes lining the Atlantic Ocean, which stretched out far and blue. She glanced at the weathered, gray-shingled buildings as she drove down narrow streets lined with shady elms. Promise Harbor hadn't changed much since the last time she'd been there. That had been for Allie's mom's funeral. Devon and Josh had been together then, and had come back to support Allie and her family. Josh's family and Allie's family had been close for years, their mothers best friends since childhood, and Josh had been nearly as devastated by Lily's death as Allie had.

That wasn't the most pleasant memory. And now here she was back again, this time not for a funeral but for a wedding. Allie and Josh's wedding. Funny how things could change.

She turned down Cranberry Road toward the little house where her dad still lived. She hadn't seen her dad since that last time she'd been back either. Which was sad, really. They talked once in a while on the phone, but Dad wasn't much into talking and their conversations were short and to the point. Guilt nudged her a little that she didn't keep in better touch, but on the other hand, he didn't make much effort either, and she knew he was probably relieved that she wasn't there much.

Her stomach tightened even more.

She pulled up on the narrow street in front of the house where she'd grown up. The small cottage with gray shingles and white trim around the windows was still neatly kept, the picket fence newly painted, the lawn mowed. The pink climbing roses her mother had planted still grew up the side of the house where the sidewalk disappeared around to the back. She sighed and climbed out of the car.

She hauled her suitcase out of the trunk and dragged it up the sidewalk toward the house. She expected Dad wasn't home, probably still working, but hopefully he still hid the key in the same place. There wasn't a lot of crime in Promise Harbor, and he could probably leave the doors unlocked if he wanted to. But he hadn't, and dammit, the key wasn't underneath the clay pot where it always used to be.

She straightened and pushed her hair off her face, turning it up to the warm June sun.

"Hello."

She jumped and turned to face a woman standing on the other side of the picket fence. Her smile creased a pretty face. Devon guessed her to be about fifty years old, with short, flippy blonde hair and cute rectangular glasses. "Hi."

"You must be Devon."

"I am."

"Your dad told me you were coming. I'm Susan Henderson. Your dad's neighbor. Obviously." She made a face.

"Nice to meet you, Susan." Devon tried to remember when the Faulkners had moved away.

"I have a key to the house," Susan said. "If you want to hang on a sec, I'll get it and let you in."

"Oh. Okay. Thanks."

Susan disappeared into her house. He'd given the neighbor a key. Huh. Devon waited, inhaling the scent of roses and sunshine. Susan returned a minute later and handed the key over the fence.

"There you go. Your dad stopped leaving a key out after some robberies happened in town."

"Robberies?" Maybe Promise Harbor *had* changed.

Susan lifted a shoulder. "Mostly tourist related. But still. You need to be careful."

"Yes," Devon agreed, approaching her to take the key. Now she was closer, she saw faint lines around the eyes that made her think maybe Susan was a little older than she'd thought at first, although she did have lovely smooth skin and rounded cheeks that gave her a youthful look. "I guess Dad's still at work."

"He should be home soon."

Devon lifted one eyebrow. Susan seemed to know a lot about what went on with Dad. Including having a key to his

26

house. "Great. I'll take my stuff in. Thanks again." She smiled politely.

She let herself into the house through the back door and walked into the kitchen. Wow. She almost had to close her eyes against the memories that flooded back. But even though some of the memories weren't that good, she felt a strange sense of comfort being in the house with which she was so familiar.

Nothing major had changed. Old-fashioned and a little more worn, the place was still neat and clean. A small African violet in a pretty pot sat on the window sill above the sink. Devon had washed many dishes at that sink, and there had never been a plant there before. The scent of cranberry filled the air, and she tracked it to a fat, red candle on the kitchen table. That was new too.

She dragged her suitcase to her bedroom. Here, things hadn't changed at all. She'd left ten years ago for college. She'd been back since then, of course, and had made some changes herself, but the same blue flowered duvet covered the twin bed, the same white blinds hung in the window, the same little white lamp sat on the painted white nightstand. And yet...there was another candle sitting on the dresser, this one blue and scented with something lovely and floral.

She was pretty sure Dad hadn't put that candle in there.

She unpacked a few things, mostly to keep busy. She should hang up her wedding dress—gah! She went very still and closed her eyes as one of those stupid stabs of pain in her chest hit again. Her dress wasn't a wedding dress. It was just a dress to wear to a wedding. Josh's wedding.

She'd spent a fortune on the damn Badgley Mischka dress. It was so beautiful.

But she hadn't known she was going to lose her job when she'd bought it. It was too late to return it, so she was stuck with it. She set her shoes—also expensive—on the floor of the closet and hung up a couple of other things. She hadn't brought much, since she only planned on staying a few days. The wedding was Saturday, and she planned to leave first thing Sunday morning for Greenbush Island. She couldn't afford to stay in the luxury resort William Mudge was staying in, but she could go hang out there and take the late ferry back to Promise Harbor.

The last few weeks had been exhausting. She hadn't slept at night and had spent her days job hunting. Her so-called friends had pretty much disappeared when they'd learned she lost her job, as if they were afraid her misfortune was contagious. Rejection sucked the life out of a person, and she'd spent her evenings watching horrid reality TV shows, eating ice cream and drinking a lot of wine.

So, yeah, really looking forward to the wedding now.

Fuck my life.

She heard a car pull in to the driveway and a door slam. Dad. She drew back her shoulders, pasted a smile on her face and headed out to greet him.

God, he looked as happy to see her as she did to be there, his weathered, tanned face tight, his eyes narrowed. "Hi, Devon."

"Hi, Dad." She moved toward him and they exchanged a brief, barely touching hug. As she drew away, his eyes flickered and she almost thought his hands trembled a little. Could he be...nervous?

"Did you get the key from Susan?" he asked.

"No, I broke in."

He didn't appreciate her attempt at humor, since he didn't laugh.

"Yes, I did," she said with an inward sigh. "She seems like a nice neighbor."

He shrugged and avoided her gaze. "I guess. She offered to watch for you since I'd be at work. And there've been some robberies in town, so I don't like leaving a key out anymore."

"Susan mentioned that," she said. "I almost came down to the office. I knew where you'd be."

Dad ran a charter fishing company. He owned a couple of boats and took people out fishing for bass and bluefish. He didn't make much money, but he loved the ocean and being outside and on the water a lot. After Mom had left, he'd spent even more time there. And less time with Devon.

"How was your drive?" he asked.

They made superficial small talk. And then a knock at the door sounded and Susan's face appeared in the window. She held a large casserole dish.

Dad moved to let her in, and she greeted him with a smile that immediately had Devon's female senses tingling. "Hello again," Susan said. She held up the covered dish. "I brought over a homemade seafood lasagna for your first evening back."

"Oh." Devon just blinked at her. "Wow. That's so nice of you."

She looked back and forth between Susan and Dad as Dad took the dish and set it on the counter.

"Thanks," he said, with a quick glance at Susan and, holy shnikes, a smile.

"I thought you might want something better than a frozen dinner like you usually eat for Devon's first night home."

When Dad and Susan looked at each other there was no mistaking the connection between them, and Devon's jaw went a little slack. Whoa. Weird.

"Uh...it smells great," she managed to say. "And I'm starving." She wasn't. She hadn't been starving since she'd gotten that wedding invitation in the mail, but they didn't need to know that. Was Susan going to stay and eat with them?

As Devon and Susan both moved at the same time to the cupboard where the plates were kept, she got her answer. Apparently Susan *was* going to stay and eat with them, without even a direct invitation from Dad. Apparently it was just assumed she'd stay for dinner. Again, whoa.

She and Susan both hesitated. Awkward! They eyed each other. Clearly Susan was comfortable here in Dad's kitchen. Susan stepped back and beamed the smile again. As Devon lifted plates out of the cupboard, Susan found cutlery and they quickly set the table, then sat down to eat.

"So your friends are getting married this weekend," Susan said. "This wedding has been the talk of the town for weeks."

"Oh. Really."

"The Ralstons and the Brewsters have been such close friends for years. It's just so romantic that they're now going to be joined by marriage. Everyone thinks so."

Everyone but Devon.

Susan clearly didn't realize that she and Josh had once been...together. Her throat tightened and she looked down at her plate of lasagna, which was actually really delicious, with chunks of shrimp and scallops and crab, and melty cheese.

Yes, Josh and Allie's families were close. Allie's mom, Lily, and Josh's mom, Sophie, had been best friends, and their kids had grown up together. Devon had met Josh through Allie when she and Allie became friends as teenagers, although their first meetings had been really nothing. He was three years older than they were, a senior in high school. The first time Devon had met him had been one Christmas, at a big, two-family get-together.

She'd immediately developed a crush on him, which she didn't even share with Allie because it was just so...crazy. He was gorgeous, six feet tall with spectacular shoulders, a football player on the school team. He had dark brown hair, eyes the color of whiskey and a wide, easy smile, and at that time a beautiful, blonde, cheerleader girlfriend who spent the holiday draped over him like the garland on the Christmas tree. So really, there wasn't even a smidgen of hope that Devon would ever get together with him. She just liked watching him and listening to him talk and worshipping him from afar. At the time she didn't think he even noticed her, but she found out later—years later—that he had.

She saw him around school occasionally, and sometimes at the Ralston home when she was there visiting Allie and he happened to be there too. He'd gone away to college in Boston the year after that, and he'd come home for Thanksgiving and Christmas and a few other occasions over the years. She'd had other boyfriends, and it wasn't as if she spent years mooning after Josh Brewster, but every time she saw him she felt a tug of attraction and a squeeze of lust that she always hid from Allie. From everybody.

"That Josh Brewster is such a nice boy," Susan continued. "Everyone in town loves him, especially after he rescued the Cardwell children from their home when it caught on fire. He's so brave."

Devon murmured her agreement, still staring down at her food.

"And everyone admires the way he looks after his family. His mom and his sister. And truthfully, he does a lot for the Ralston family too, since Lily passed away."

Of course he did.

"And Allie is so beautiful," Susan chatted on. "They make such a gorgeous couple. I hear her wedding dress is spectacular."

"Allie always did like pretty clothes," Devon murmured.

When Devon had moved to Boston to go to college, Josh

had graduated with a degree in fire science and was working with the Boston Fire Department. Allie had contacted him and asked him to call Devon to see how she was doing in the big city all on her own. The first time she'd heard his voice on the phone, she'd gone all sticky-tongued, her heart hammering. He'd suggested meeting for coffee sometime, and at first she tried to decline, but he insisted that Allie wanted him to see her and see how she was doing, so she agreed.

After that first coffee together, they hadn't seen each other much, but Josh had kept in touch and helped her out with so many things, looking after her in the big city. She'd told herself he was like a big brother and pushed away those feelings of attraction for him. Until one day...things had changed.

Devon poked at her lasagna as Susan talked. Dad made brief, unhelpful responses as Devon drifted off into memory land. That first time Josh had kissed her was a memory she liked to pull out every once in a while and relive, a memory that made her heart both fill with joy and ache with sadness. It was kind of like when you had something stuck in your tooth, or a canker sore that you just couldn't leave alone, even though it hurt. She kept that memory alive and well even though it...hurt. She guessed the word would be *bittersweet.* Kind of like coming to his wedding, with a bride who wasn't her.

She was brought back to the present by the peculiar sight of her father and Susan talking and smiling at each other. After they'd eaten, Devon went do the dishes as she always had as a teenager, and Susan stayed in the kitchen to help. Dad left them alone, and she heard the television in the living room come on.

She shot Susan a glance as she squeezed some dish soap into the sink. "Have you lived next door long?"

Susan looked at her and gave a crooked smile. "Doug hasn't told you about me, has he?"

"Um. No." They didn't talk much, and when they did it

wasn't much beyond the basics. A relationship with a woman, though? Hell, that was something to mention. You would think.

Susan smiled. "Well, I'll leave that to him."

"Ha," Devon said. "You might as well tell me. Apparently he isn't going to."

Susan lifted an eyebrow, and guilt nudged Devon for being so disloyal to her father as to criticize him to a stranger.

"Dad's been alone a long time," she said. "I guess I'm just a little surprised."

"He told me about your mother leaving."

"Yes. That was sixteen years ago."

Devon understood why her mom had left. She'd been beautiful and fun, and Devon had always known her mom had wanted more than living in Promise Harbor, married to a man who ran a little charter fishing business. She liked to dress up and go out for dinner, and although there were some lovely restaurants in Promise Harbor that catered to the huge influx of tourists every summer, she'd always wanted to go to Boston or New York to shop and dine and go to plays and concerts. That wasn't exactly Dad's kind of thing.

Even as a kid Devon had wondered how they'd gotten together, and later in life she figured it out between the pieces she knew, the small things her dad shared and what she learned from others in the town. Her mom's family was wealthy and had owned a summer property just outside town, and the summer she'd been eighteen, she'd met Dad. They'd fallen in love and her mom got pregnant. With her. Somehow Mom ended up staying in Promise Harbor and stayed for twelve years that apparently were torture for her. Eventually she just couldn't do it anymore and returned to her family in New York, to the life they wanted her to lead.

What Devon didn't understand then, and probably never would, was why her mom hadn't taken her with her.

"That must have been difficult," Susan said in a gentle voice. "I can't imagine leaving my children."

"You have children?"

"Yes. They're both away at college." In answer to the questioning look Devon flashed her, she added, "I'm divorced."

Devon nodded. "I'm sorry."

"No. It's a good thing, believe me. But when my husband and I split up, I would have fought to the death to keep my kids with me."

Devon bent her head and scrubbed at a plate.

Why hadn't her mom taken her with her?

She'd asked herself that question a million times. She'd wanted to go with her. Not that she didn't love her dad. But a girl wants her mother, and she'd always loved it when her mom took her on those big-city trips. She was fascinated by her mom's family's life, by the big city, by skyscrapers and boutiques and elegant restaurants. She wanted that too, and when her mom had left to resume that life without her, she'd been devastated.

The day Mom had left, Devon had cried and begged her to take her with her. Her mom had told her to stop crying because she looked awful. So she'd swallowed hard, wiped her tears and tried to smile. But her mom had left without her anyway. After that, Devon had that vowed nobody would ever see her cry again.

Now, she only had contempt for a mother who could do something like that, but at the time, she'd known her mother was leaving her because she wasn't good enough to fit into that life. Neither was her dad, with his sun- and windburned face, calloused hands and worn work clothes. So they had to stay together while Mom went to live the life she'd always wanted.

"Your father is a good man," Susan said. "I suppose your mom knew that she could trust him to look after you."

Devon's chest ached. Sure, Dad was a good man. And yes, he'd looked after her. But there'd been a lot missing from her life.

"My dad changed after my mom left," she said quietly. "He was never one to talk a lot, kind of the strong, silent type, you know?"

Susan smiled and nodded and picked up a towel to dry the plates she'd just washed.

"He used to talk more, though. And laugh, and smile. But after my mom left...he didn't smile much anymore."

He'd lifted his chin, squared his shoulders and told Devon she'd have to help with meals and chores more. She'd tried to talk to him, to ask him what had happened. She wanted...*needed* to know it wasn't her fault Mom had left. But he refused to talk about it, and their life continued as it always had but without the vibrant fun and glamour Mom had brought into it, instead becoming dull and gray.

She didn't tell Susan all that, though. Telling people about stuff like that was uncomfortable. She'd never wanted people to feel sorry for her, so she always pretended things were fine and never complained or whined. She never cried. She just carried on, like Dad wanted her to.

The only person who knew about that was Allie. When Devon had started hanging around with her, Allie's family had dazzled her. They talked and laughed and did fun things together. They put up a Christmas tree and decorated it every year, and they baked birthday cakes for every birthday and had parties even for the adults. She was sure they felt sorry for her, for the way her mom had left and the way her dad treated her. Not that he treated her badly—it wasn't abuse or anything—but eating frozen turkey and stuffing dinners on Christmas day with no Christmas decorations whatsoever was pretty pathetic.

But as with everything else, she pretended she was fine.

Chapter Three

Josh squinted at the label on the beer bottle he held, trying to focus his eyes on it with considerable difficulty. "Is this beer really called Bromance?" he asked Jackson, his best friend and the best man at his wedding tomorrow. They'd been sitting in Stone's Sports Bar for the last...how long? Josh had lost track, and all his other buddies had headed home. Only he and Jackson were left after going out with the guys the night before the wedding.

"Yes. Bromance Brown Ale."

Josh nodded. "Okay. Good. I love you, man."

"Maybe time to get you home," Jackson said.

"No. I don't wanna go home yet."

"Why not?"

Josh now tried to focus on the wood grain of the small table. How could he tell Jackson the truth? He didn't want to go home because then he'd go to bed and fall asleep—or pass out—and when he woke up it would be his wedding day.

"I might be having cold feet," he mumbled.

Jackson leaned closer. "What's that? What'd you say?"

Josh sighed. "I might be having cold feet."

Jackson's eyebrows flew up. "About the wedding?"

"No, about getting up from this table." Then he laughed loudly. Damn, he was funny. Drunk, but funny.

"Shit, man, are you serious? You want to back out of the wedding?"

"No. Of course not. I wouldn't do that."

Jackson eyed him. "But you have doubts."

Josh sighed. "Doesn't every guy before he straps on the old ball and chain?" Then he slumped a little. He'd never thought of Allie as a "ball and chain" and that was really unfair. She was awesome and he wanted to marry her. He did. "Didn't mean that," he mumbled.

"I guess some guys do." Jackson grimaced and shoved a hand through his hair. "I've never had the guts to even propose to someone, so I wouldn't know. But yeah, it's probably normal to feel a little nervous about it. It's a big step. It's serious."

"Yeah. Serious. You're not helping, dude."

Jackson grinned. "Sorry. Okay, how's this. You've known Allie forever. You love her. You love her family. They love you. Your mom is thrilled to pieces about this. The whole town is behind you on this. There's nothing to be afraid of. You two are going to have a long and happy life together."

Josh nodded, still looking down at the table. "Still not helping."

Jackson gave him a hearty slap on the back, nearly knocking him off his stool. "You'll be fine. Once you're up there at the front of the church watching Allie walk down the aisle looking like a million bucks, you'll be so glad you're marrying her."

Josh picked up his Bromance Brown Ale and drained it. "Right. Absholutely. Can't wait."

"Fuck." Jackson eyed him. With all four or maybe five eyes. "You're hammered."

"No I am not." Josh straightened. "I'm fine. Let's have another round."

"Nope. I am doing my best man duty and hauling your ass out of here. You're already going to need a large bottle of Tylenol and a jug of Visine in the morning."

"Oh, all right." Josh slid off the stool and held on to the table for a moment when the floor shifted just a bit underneath his feet. Hey, was that an earthquake? If there was a major earthquake they probably wouldn't be able to have the wedding tomorrow.

That was stupid. He *wanted* to marry Allie.

"I need a burger," he announced.

Jackson rolled his eyes. "Okay, big guy. Let's head to Barney's and then I'll take you home."

"Yeah. Barney's. I can have a hickory burger. And fries." For some reason, at that moment Devon popped into his head. Sitting at Barney's Chowder House eating hickory burgers with her. That was her favorite burger too. Guess Barney's hickory burger was always going to be associated with her in his mind.

His fucked-up, shit-faced mind.

They walked the short distance from the bar to Barney's, the June evening clear and fresh. Josh took deep breaths of the faintly briny air of Promise Harbor, the Atlantic Ocean not far away no matter where you were. He loved living here, even though it had been a tough decision to move back last year. What the hell was he so worried about? Living here as a married man wasn't going to be any different than living here as a single guy.

Did that make *any* sense? Of course it would be different. He'd be *married*.

Inside Barney's, people filled nearly every booth and table. Friday night. Right. But Josh and Jackson found an empty table and took a seat.

"You know," Jackson said. "If you're seriously having doubts about getting married, it's not too late."

Josh gave him a crooked smile. "Sure it is."

"No. It's not too late until the vows are said." Jackson leaned across the table, his face serious. "If you want to run, I'll drive us to Mexico tonight. Just say the word."

"Mexico?" Josh lifted an eyebrow.

"Or wherever."

Josh shook his head. "You know I can't do that. I made a promise to Allie. I always keep my word."

"Yeah. You always do." Jackson grinned. "You are a man of honor."

"Damn right." The scent of seafood chowder, charbroiled burgers and greasy French fries filled his head and made his stomach growl. "I'm a man of honor," he told the waitress who arrived to take their order. "And I'm fucking starving."

She blinked at him.

"Don't mind him," Jackson said with a smile for the teenage girl. "He's getting married tomorrow."

"I am," he said. "To the most wonderful woman in the world."

But once again, Devon's face appeared in his mind. What the fuck? Why did he keep thinking of her tonight? Then he blinked. Blinked again. And shook his head.

He wasn't just imagining her face. She was right there in front of him, sitting in the booth across from them.

Holy fuck.

He stared at her. She stared back at him.

"Devon," he breathed.

Jackson's head snapped around. "Devon?"

Josh swallowed. His heart might have stopped. He had to get it going again or he would die. And he couldn't die the day before his wedding. But there...yeah, his heart was going again. Fast. Hard. That might be worse. Now he was afraid it was going to explode out of his chest. He looked at Jackson. "Allie invited her to the wedding."

"Jesus Christ."

She was sitting by herself in the small booth, a half-eaten hickory burger in front of her on the table, looking back at him with wide eyes and parted lips. Her long chestnut hair hung around her shoulders, and those sexy, tilted eyes blinked at him. Then she smiled, a sort of sad little smile that made him ache. "Hi, Josh."

"Devon. Hey." The next thing he knew he was sitting across from her, still staring at her. "How are you?"

Devon's throat closed up and her hands trembled, so she clasped them together in her lap beneath the table. *Why* had she come here? She'd been hanging around at home with her dad. He'd gone to bed, and she'd tried to but couldn't sleep. For some crazy reason, she'd decided to visit Barney's Chowder House and have a hickory burger. Not that she was hungry, but she loved Barney's hickory burgers and here she was in Promise Harbor, and...why not? And now Josh was sitting across from her, staring at her.

"Devon. Hey," he said. "How are you?"

"Good. I'm good. How are you?"

"Good." A pause. "I'm drunk."

"Oh. Okay." A smile tugged her lips. Jeebus Crust, he was so damn gorgeous he made her heart constrict. His dark brown hair was standing on end in every direction, and his golden-brown eyes gazed back at her with somewhat unfocused intensity. A scruff of beard darkened his square jaw, and his wide mouth curved up into a sheepish smile. "I guess that's allowed the night before your wedding."

"Yeah." His eyes shadowed. "I'm getting married tomorrow,

Devon."

"I know. That's why I'm here." Her heart now softened, looking at his long lashes lowering over amber eyes, his short, straight nose, his beautiful mouth. Images bombarded her—her stroking a finger down his nose, kissing the corners of that mouth, running her hands through his hair, nuzzling his neck, breathing in his scent.

He tipped his head to one side. "I didn't think you would come."

Her chest was so tight she could hardly breathe. "Well. Um. I wanted to come and...and wish you a-and A-Allie all the best." She *hated* how her voice stuttered.

He nodded slowly, his face solemn. "Really?"

No. "Yes."

"Have you seen Allie?"

"No." She didn't think she could. She hadn't thought she could face her, either. She'd pictured herself sitting in the church, just one of the two hundred or so other guests there to witness their vows. But now Josh sat right in front of her.

There was so much she wanted to say to him, and yet so much she couldn't say to him. *Josh.* Pressure built behind her eyes and cheekbones. Emotion swelled inside her. *Why are you marrying her? What about me? What happened to us, Josh? What is she giving you that I couldn't? Just living here in Promise Harbor? Is that it?*

After Josh had left, after she'd cried for about a week and spent the next six months wavering between anger and depression, she'd told herself that someday she would meet someone else. Someone like him. Someone honorable and brave and loyal. There was another man out there, someone like him, but someone who'd honor *her*, someone who'd be loyal to *her*.

Her heart hurt so badly at that moment she couldn't think straight. They were sitting there staring at each other across the small table in Barney's Chowder House, where they'd come that time they'd been back in Promise Harbor for Allie's mom's funeral, the only time they'd ever been there as a couple. The air around them thickened, heavy with memories, longing and regrets. Well, *she* felt regrets anyway—she couldn't speak for Josh, but as he looked at her with heavy-lidded eyes and a slow, wistful smile...she thought maybe he did too.

But it was too late for that, so she pushed that all to the back of her brain where it belonged. Later she would pull out the memories again, let herself feel the longing and regrets, but now, she couldn't. Because tomorrow Josh and Allie were getting married.

Her throat closed up and her eyes burned but she kept that smile firmly in place, trying to show him she was okay. "I hope you and Allie will be very happy together," she said, her voice low because if she spoke any louder it would come out shaky. "I want you to be happy."

She really did want him to be happy. Even though *she* wasn't.

"Devon." Her name was a sigh across his lips.

Jackson was sitting there watching them, his eyebrows pinched together. Devon smiled at him too, and he kind of winced. The waitress arrived with their burgers and fries. "Your food's there," she said, nodding.

"Uh. Yeah." Josh hesitated. "Want to join us?"

Her smile started to hurt. "No, I'm done. I'm just leaving. Nice to see you again, Josh."

Still he looked at her with that funny expression, and then he too smiled and nodded. "You too, Devon. You too."

She grabbed her bill and hurried to the front to pay it so she could get the hell out of there.

"Dearly beloved, we are gathered here today to unite this man and this woman in holy matrimony." The minister's voice carried through the hushed church as the ceremony began. Reverend Morgan opened his mouth to continue—

"Oh, hell no."

Every head in St. Mark's Methodist Church swiveled toward the man striding down the center aisle. Dressed in a hooded sweatshirt and T-shirt over faded jeans, he did not fit in. At all.

Sitting there with the rest of the wedding guests, Devon's eyes nearly popped out of her head. Was that Gavin Montgomery, unshaven and shaggy-haired? She almost didn't recognize him.

Hayley Stone, sitting next to Devon, leaped to her feet. Devon frowned as a small twig and a leaf fell from Hayley's hair at her abrupt movement.

"*Gavin?*" The bride's shocked question rose above the gasps, whispers and creaking pews in the church.

Jeebus Crust, had Allie invited both her *and* Josh's exes to their wedding? That took guts. Except...what was Gavin doing?

"This is *Gavin?*" Josh glanced incredulously at Allie. He turned back to Gavin and took a step toward him, frowning. "What the hell do you think you're doing?"

Oh yeah. The entire congregation wanted to know the answer to that question, including Devon.

"I'm here to talk to Allie," Gavin said.

Josh shoved his way between him and Allie. "We're kind of in the middle of something."

Devon watched Josh step so protectively in front of his fiancée. *His fiancée.* An ache developed behind her breastbone and she pressed a hand there.

"Yeah, this can't wait." Gavin looked past Josh to Allie. "I need to talk to you. Now."

Allie's face blanched and her eyes went wide. Devon almost jumped up to go to her, thinking she might be about to pass out. Greta, Josh's sister and Allie's matron of honor, stepped closer. Something twinged inside Devon that might have been...jealousy. She'd always thought *she* would be Allie's maid of honor. Not that she wanted to be. Not at *this* wedding.

Gavin started to move toward Allie, but Josh blocked him. "I don't think so, Gavin."

The church was completely silent. The man in front of Devon had his phone out and was snapping pictures, for god's sake. He'd probably be posting them on Facebook next. Devon leaned forward. "Stop that!" she hissed.

"Listen, I can do this here in front of the whole town." Gavin said. "I don't mind. I'm leaving here with Allie one way or another. But I think keeping some of this private might be appropriate." He leaned around Josh to look at Allie. "I have some things I need to say before you say I do to another man, Al."

Josh sighed, stepped closer and lowered his voice. Openmouthed, Devon strained to hear his words. "Don't do this, Gavin. Haven't you messed with her enough? Just let her be happy."

"That's exactly what I want to do," Gavin said, his voice firm. "Is that what *you* want?"

"I'm standing next to her in a tux in front of a minister. What do you think?"

Devon stared at Josh, his short, dark brown hair combed so neatly back from his face, his square jaw clean-shaven and—right now—clenched tight. Yes, he was standing there in a tux, so elegant and handsome, ready to marry another woman. He didn't look happy about this interruption. Good god, how humiliating to have another man interrupt your wedding vows! Devon again resisted the urge to leap to her feet and this time rush to *his* side. Her hands gripped the back of the pew in front of her as she slid to the edge of the seat.

"I think that if you don't let her talk to me, you know that she'll always wonder. You don't want that, do you? To have your wife wondering about another man?"

Josh blew out a long breath and shoved his hand through his hair. Then he half turned to his bride. "Allie?"

"What would I wonder?" Allie asked, looking at Gavin.

"You'd wonder what I had to say to you so badly that I would fly over four thousand miles so I could rush in here to stop your wedding."

Allie stared at Gavin. There wasn't a sound in the church as time stretched out.

Devon could not believe this. Wide-eyed, she gazed at the scene unfolding, waiting along with everyone else in the church for Allie's response. It was as if the entire congregation held their collective breath.

"Allie," Gavin said again, breaking the silence.

Allie pressed her lips together and shook her head. "You're too late," she whispered.

Devon exhaled slowly. But in the candlelit sanctuary, tears gleamed in Allie's eyes. Why was she crying? She should be pissed at Gavin for doing this, interrupting their wedding. Devon's gaze shifted to Josh. Now *he* looked pissed. Oh god. If he really loved Allie, this would be breaking his heart. Her own heart constricted for him, and she lifted a hand to her throat.

"Bullshit," Gavin said. He stepped forward, bent his knees and lifted Allie into his arms. He headed for the side door of the church. A murmur swept through the congregation.

"Gavin!" Allie kicked the skirt of her wedding dress tangled around her legs, but he didn't stop.

"Just a damn minute—" Josh started.

Gavin turned. "Give me a chance," Gavin said to Josh. "Let me talk to her. Let me tell her what I came here to say. Then if she wants to come back, I'll walk her down the aisle myself."

Gavin turned back to the door, bending his head to say something to Allie. She gazed up at him and whispered something back. Mrs. Gurney, the pianist, sprang to open the door, and Gavin stepped out into the June sunshine with Josh's bride in his arms.

Devon's mouth dropped open again. Oh dear god. Devon looked back at Josh, at the grim line of his mouth, his eyebrows drawn down over his beautiful amber eyes. And then, as he turned to look at the crowded church, her eye caught his. And held. Heat burst inside her, and she once again nearly leaped to her feet to go to him.

Then he turned and strode to the door to follow them outside. Sunlight filled the church as the door opened, then closed behind him, leaving a stunned crowd sitting there amid the scent of beeswax and flowers. Holy fishsticks.

This time she couldn't stop herself. She rose and began to squeeze past the others in the pew. "Excuse me," she whispered. "Excuse me. Oh, sorry! Excuse me."

People had started to whisper and buzz, and she hurried over to the side door Josh had just walked out of. She blinked in the sun, then focused on Josh, who stood on the sidewalk, yelling, "Wait!"

Gavin stopped and turned, still holding a big poof of white wedding dress that was Allie.

"What the fuck, Allie?" Josh demanded. "Are you leaving with him?"

Gavin gave Josh a direct look. "Allie called me last night," he said.

Josh froze. "You did?"

Allie opened her mouth to reply, blinking rapidly, but no

words came out.

"She called and told me that she'd always love me," Gavin added.

In Gavin's arms, Allie groaned and closed her eyes.

"Allie? Is this true?"

Finally she said softly, "Well..."

Gavin smirked.

Josh's hands curled into fists. He shook his head. "Jesus Christ. Were you drunk?"

Her eyes shifted away from his. "Maybe a little."

Meep. Devon recalled that Josh had been more than a little toasted last night too.

"You called Gavin the night before our wedding and told him you'd always love him?"

"Not exactly," she said. "I didn't tell him to come or anything. I didn't *say* that I loved him."

Josh pinched the bridge of his nose. "Allie. We're getting married. You don't just change your mind at the last second about something like this."

"I'm sorry," she whispered.

Josh continued to stand there, his shoulders rigid.

Oh my god. This was really happening. Devon's heart knocked against her breastbone.

Allie looked up at Gavin and nodded. "That's all I needed to hear," he said, and turned and marched to his vehicle, parked at an angle in the loading zone in front of the church as if he'd raced up at sixty miles an hour.

Josh rubbed the back of his neck and looked down at his shoes, then turned. Leaning against the church door, Devon's eyes met his. "Devon," he murmured.

"Is she really leaving with him?" she demanded.

He nodded.

"Shnikes. Are you okay?"

"Yeah." He scowled. "I'm pissed as hell but I'm okay. What the fuck, Dev? I just got left at the altar."

"I can't believe that." She studied his face. He definitely seemed more angry than heartbroken.

"I know! I can't believe that asshole just stormed in there like that."

"What a shitty thing to do."

"And I can't believe she left with him. Jesus fucking Christ." He rubbed the back of his head. "When you give someone your word and say you're going to do it, you fucking well *do* it."

"Yes." She gave him a sad smile. "You do." Oh yeah. That was Josh, all right. A man of his word.

He shook his head. "What the hell am I supposed to do now? There's a whole church full of people sitting in there. This is unbelievable."

Her heart ached for him. "I guess you better go in and tell them the wedding's off."

"Fuck." He closed his eyes and leaned his head back for a moment. "Yeah. I guess I'd better."

Chapter Four

His mother had insisted that they have the reception, but she'd also insisted that Josh should be going after Allie. And he was starting to think so too. He leaned against the bar in the banquet room of the Promise Harbor Inn, a beer in his hand, watching the guests mingle, drinking champagne and eating hors d'oeuvres.

Jesus, Allie was crazy to go off with that guy! What kind of douche bag walked into someone's wedding and practically kidnapped the bride?

His eyes fell on Police Detective Hayley Stone, talking to Jackson. Apparently she'd come as his date. How the hell that had happened, Josh had no clue. As of yesterday, Jackson had been fighting off puck bunnies and planning to attend the wedding alone. For a moment Josh contemplated going over to Hayley and asking her to get involved. Maybe they should send the cops after Allie and Gavin. The guy must be deranged and possibly dangerous.

But where would he be taking her? Josh pulled out his cell phone, thumbed through his contacts to find Allie's number and pressed the button to call her one more time. Still no answer. "Shit."

"You okay?"

He turned to once again see Devon. Her chestnut hair glinted red in the light of the chandeliers, and her tilted, almond-shaped eyes were shadowed with concern.

"I'm okay," he muttered. "But I'm worried about Allie."

"Really?" She lifted an eyebrow. "She just jilted you in front of all these people, and you're worried about her?" Then she laughed and shook her head. "What am I saying? Of course you are."

He scowled. "Who knows what Gavin's doing with her," he growled. "He could be baked as a cake, on drugs or something, knowing him."

Devon choked on a laugh. "I don't think he's that bad." She laid a hand on his arm and gave a gentle squeeze through the fabric of his tux jacket.

Huh. He looked down at her hand on his arm and swallowed. "I should go after her," he said. "Except I have no idea where they went."

"Did you just try to call her?" She nodded at the cell phone still in his hand.

"Yeah. No answer."

She pursed her lips as if thinking. "I have no idea where Gavin's been living."

"Nobody else here does, either. His parents were at the church, but they didn't come to the reception."

"What about...where were you going on your honeymoon? Maybe they went there?"

"Oh for fuck's sake...they wouldn't...would they?"

She shrugged slender shoulders. "I have no idea. It was just a suggestion."

"I booked the honeymoon suite at the Oceanside Inn on Greenbush Island. It's already charged to my credit card."

Her eyes went wide. "Seriously? Greenbush Island?"

"What wrong with that? It's a nice place."

"Um. Yeah. It's a gorgeous place." She blinked. Her eyes looked away, then back at him. She bit her lip. "And it's paid for, you say?"

50

"Yeah." He grimaced.

After another short pause, she said, "I could go see if they're there."

He stared at her. "What?"

"I'll go see if they're there." She lifted one shoulder. "There's still time to get the last ferry."

"But...why would you do that?"

A smile flickered on her beautiful mouth. "Just trying to help."

Thoughts jumbled up in his head. He needed to do something, to try to find Allie, to make sure she was okay. But this was Devon standing there in front of him, still so beautiful, offering to help him. Devon.

When he'd seen her last night at Barney's Chowder House, he'd been stupefied. Dazzled. Blown away. He'd been drunk too, but the truth was, he'd been thinking about her before he'd even seen her. Thinking about the woman he'd loved and lost the night before his wedding. And now she was offering to go to Greenbush Island to try to find Allie.

"Okay," he said. He set down his beer and slipped his phone back into his pocket. "Let's go."

She froze. "You're coming with me?"

"Yeah. Why not?" He glanced around the room. "This isn't exactly a fun night for me. Let's go."

Devon's heart bumped in her chest. It was a bat-shit crazy thing to suggest, and even crazier to actually do it. She'd thought she could go over to the island to see if Gavin and Allie had checked into the honeymoon suite, which they probably had not, in which case *she* would check in and then hang around and see if she could bump into William Mudge and...

51

But she never anticipated that Josh would want to come with her. Holy fishsticks.

He grabbed her hand and started tugging her toward one of the doors. "Should you tell someone where we're going?" she asked, tripping along after him in her spiky heels.

He paused. "Yeah. I'll tell Jackson." He looked around, and Devon followed his gaze to where Jackson stood across the room, talking to Hayley Stone. "Be right back."

She watched him stride across the room and pause beside his best man. The two of them made a picture, both so tall and gorgeous in their dark tuxes. Josh spoke to Jackson briefly, gave his shoulder a squeeze, then turned and met her eyes as he walked back toward her. She swallowed.

"Okay, let's go." Instead of heading to the lobby, he led her down a hall in the other direction, and pushed through a door that opened directly into the parking lot the banquet room overlooked. She cast a glance at the windows. Was anyone watching them make their exit like this?

"My...my car." She blinked. "I parked over there." She lifted her chin.

"Okay. Get your car. Go home and get your stuff. Meet me at the ferry as soon as you can."

"You can't be serious."

He gave her a mirthless smile. "Serious as a five-alarm fire, honey."

Still she paused. Then, "Okay. I'll meet you there in about half an hour."

He nodded, squeezed the hand he still held and met her eyes. "Thanks, Dev."

Devon had no idea what she was going to tell her father when she went home to get her things, but it turned out she didn't have to tell him anything because he wasn't there. She paused in the kitchen after letting herself in the back door. He was probably next door at Susan's. She could go over there and see and tell him she was leaving.

But she took the cowardly way out instead and left a note on the kitchen counter.

Dad:

You probably heard about the wedding. It's off. So I'm going home. I'll give you a call. Thanks for letting me stay. See you soon.

She packed up the few things she had brought with her, jumped into her car and drove to the wharf where the ferry for Greenbush Island departed. For a moment she contemplated changing direction, hitting I-93 and heading back to Boston. But dammit, William Mudge was on that island.

William Mudge, director of human resources at Heffington International. One more verging-on-desperate chance to get her precious career—and her life—back on track before people found out about her embarrassing unemployment. She did *not* need people feeling sorry for her.

So she drove to the wharf and parked in the lot, assuming they would take Josh's car on the ferry.

But where was Josh? For a brief moment, a flash of hope that he wouldn't show up zipped through her. Because this was crazy. But that was stupid. If there was a man on this planet whom you could count on to do what he said he would, it was Josh Brewster.

And yeah, there he was. He had a duffel bag sitting on the ground beside him where he leaned up against a fence, looking at his phone and frowning. She grabbed her suitcase and dragged it across the parking lot through the lowering afternoon sun.

He looked up and saw her and his frown relaxed into a crooked smile. "Hey. You came."

"Did you think I wouldn't?"

His eyes shadowed. "My track record of being stood up isn't so good today."

Yeah, true that. "I'm sorry, Josh." It wasn't her fault, but she was sorry...sorry that he'd been embarrassed, inconvenienced...heartbroken? She studied his face.

"Don't worry about it." His phone buzzed and he frowned as he glanced at it. He rolled his eyes.

"Who is it?"

"Allie's brother. People keep calling me to see where I am and if I've found Allie yet."

"How do they know you're looking for her?"

"I called my mother. I knew she'd wonder where I was. I told her I'm trying to find Allie. That made her happy."

Devon's stomach tightened. "I guess she was pretty happy you two were getting married."

"Ecstatic." Josh's mouth thinned into a flat line. "So she's glad I'm trying to rescue her from being kidnapped."

Devon's mouth fell open. "Kidnapped? People think she's been kidnapped?"

"You know how rumors get started in this town." He rubbed his face. "I told her Allie left of her own free will, but even so, people make up their own versions of what happened."

"I guess everyone's worried about her."

"Yeah. Hence all the phone calls."

The truth was, *Devon* was a little worried about Allie. Running away with Gavin like that was something so impulsive and crazy and so unlike Allie, it was no wonder everyone had been in shock. What had gotten into her? Although Gavin was known by many in Promise Harbor, he'd been gone for a long time and was primarily now known as the man who'd broken Allie Ralston's heart. He hadn't even showed up when Allie's mom had died, for the love of Jeebus. Why on earth would she go with him like that? She'd thrown away marriage to the most decent, loyal, honorable man there was to run away with a guy who'd been nothing but trouble.

They left her car on the mainland and took Josh's vehicle onto the ferry. After parking, they climbed out and joined other passengers on the deck of the ferry as the boat glided away from the wharf and slowly moved out into the channel toward Greenbush Island.

Devon leaned against the railing, the ocean breeze tossing her hair around her face. She pulled strands away from her mouth and held them at her nape with one hand, watching the town of Promise Harbor recede as they chugged out of the cove.

Josh leaned beside her and she glanced at his profile: the short, straight nose that gave him a boyish look, the strong jaw, his long eyelashes. Something stirred inside her, a flutter of attraction, a curl of heat, along with sympathy. Damn. She'd felt it that night at Barney's too.

Josh had broken her heart, something that had taken her a long time to get over. Coming back here had been meant to prove to everyone, and hopefully to herself, that she'd gotten over him, that she'd moved on with her life. But the way her insides tightened when she looked at him, the way her body tingled, the way her heart ached thinking about him being hurt, told her she wasn't over him.

Which only meant this was an even worse idea. Helping Josh find his fiancée? Yeah, that sounded like a lot of fun.

At that moment, Devon was tempted to climb over the railing, jump off the boat and swim to shore. Her heart picked up speed and her breathing went shallow as anxiety gripped her. What the hell was she doing?

She forced herself to breathe normally, drawing air into her lungs slowly, fresh, briny sea air, forced herself to relax her death grip on the railing. William Mudge. The position at Heffington International. The job she so badly needed, not just to pay her rent, although yeah, that was pretty damn important, but because her career was who she *was*. It was, sadly, all she had. So, *that* was what she was doing. This was going to work out perfectly. She stole a glance at Josh.

What if they found Allie there? Then what would they do? Was Josh going to try to fight for her? This could get ugly.

But what if they didn't find Allie? She had no idea what would happen then.

Josh leaned on the rail beside her, and they both stared out at the ocean, undulating in shades of gray and blue, creamy whitecaps dotting the surface here and there. Seagulls soared above, the lowering sun illuminating them, pure white against the clear blue sky.

"So," Devon said. "You and Allie planned to spend your honeymoon on the island."

"I planned it," he said. "I just told her about it yesterday so she'd know what to pack."

"Oh. That's a beautiful inn."

"Yeah." He lifted one big shoulder. "I thought it would be nice. Not too far away. And there are lots of things to do on the island."

Devon pursed her lips. On a honeymoon, you wouldn't think they'd care about things to do—beyond getting out of bed to answer the door for room service. But what did she know about honeymoons? Nothing, that's what.

"I haven't been over here for years," she said.

Josh's phone buzzed again.

"Oh for Chrissake," he muttered. "I feel like tossing this

thing overboard."

"Um. That's an expensive-looking phone."

"Yeah." He sighed. "And I need to keep it on in case anything comes up at work." After a brief pause, he added, "Or if Allie calls."

"So if a fire breaks out, you might have to interrupt your honeymoon to go put it out?"

He turned and looked at her, and she caught the glimmer of humor in his amber eyes. "I'm not on my honeymoon."

"True." Her own lips quirked. "You know what I meant."

"Yeah." A smile ghosted over his lips. "I doubt if I'd have to go fight a fire, but I'm a shift captain, and you never know what might come up."

"I didn't know you were a captain. Congratulations."

"Thanks."

"When did that happen?"

"A few months ago."

"Do you like it?" Devon studied his face. "It must seem awfully tame after what you were doing in Boston."

Josh had graduated at the top of his class in college, and it hadn't taken him long with the Boston Fire Department to work his way into the special operations command. That was the department responsible for all the special rescue services for the fire department, things like confined space rescue, structural collapse rescue, hazardous materials and decontamination operations and a whole lot of other scary things she couldn't even remember.

"I do like it," he said slowly. "Yeah, it's different. But I've worked my way up, and I like being a captain and having more responsibility. Chief Langley is retiring in a couple of years, and I might have a shot at being chief."

"That would be awesome. And not surprising at all."

He gave her a look. "Thanks."

"What was the look for?"

"What look?"

"The look. You know. Like you're surprised I'd compliment you."

He grimaced and looked away. "Maybe I am."

She went silent. She chewed a little on her bottom lip. Why would he think that? He had to know how much she admired him—his bravery, his dedication to his career, the way he put himself on the line to save other people. He was like a superhero to her. He'd been like a superhero to her since the day she'd met him, and after he'd become a firefighter she'd been even more in awe of him.

She just wished he'd been a superhero for *her.*

A wave of sadness washed over her, as if the Atlantic had surged up over the ferry. She sighed. "Yeah, you're just a big loser jerk," she said.

He laughed. She loved the sound of that. It was the first time she'd heard him laugh since she'd been back in Promise Harbor. She wanted to make him laugh more.

They'd always laughed a lot, she and Josh. Until things had gotten messed up back in Promise Harbor and Josh had been tense and then she'd been tense and...well. It hadn't ended well.

"Want to get a coffee?" he asked.

"Yeah. Sure."

They spent the rest of the ferry ride buying coffees, then sitting on a bench at the back of the ferry, drinking them, watching as the sun lowered toward the mainland. The low light shone into her eyes and warmed her, seeping into her bones even though the ocean breeze cooled her cheeks. Josh's phone kept buzzing, and he kept looking at it with a scowl, but he didn't answer it.

Greenbush Island was a popular tourist spot in the summer, not as well known as the Vineyard or Nantucket, but becoming a fashionable destination for well-to-do tourists. Like William Mudge and his family. The beaches were pristine and serene, with some protected local plant species. There were a couple of small towns on the island, and a number of luxury hotels and inns had recently been built to take advantage of the growing tourism.

They found Josh's vehicle and waited their turn to drive off the ferry. They drove through the tiny town of Silverport. "It's not far," Josh said. "Just the other side of town. It's right on the beach."

Devon looked out the window as he drove, her stomach in a mass of knots. This was insane. But she was desperate.

Josh turned down the road to the inn, and as it came into view, she sat up straighter. So beautiful. The huge, typically gray-shingled structure had white shutters and a wide veranda stretching across the front of it. Three stories tall, it had several turrets and peaks. They drove past smooth, green lawns and carefully tended flowerbeds overflowing with lush shrubs and colorful flowers. White lampposts lined the driveway, topped with antique-looking lamps illuminating the dusk with golden light.

"Wow," she said. "Nice."

Josh just shrugged. His hands gripped the steering wheel, and she had a feeling he was just as freaked out about this as she was.

He parked at the side and they walked inside. The lobby was like an elegant living room with shiny, dark hardwood floors, white painted walls and woodwork, comfy, beige-upholstered chairs and antique tables grouped on beige rugs. Lamps glowed on the tables. A fire flickered in the big fireplace on one wall, and a dark wood railing with white spindles edged a wide staircase to a second level.

She trailed behind Josh as he approached the reception desk.

"I have a reservation," he began. "Brewster. The—"

"Honeymoon suite," said the clerk with a smile. "Your suite will be ready for you in a few minutes, Mr. Brewster. Why don't you and your bride have a seat over there and we'll come get you when it's ready."

Devon sank her teeth into her bottom lip. Holy shnikes. They thought she was the bride. Oops.

"So, uh, nobody else has checked in yet?" Josh asked.

The clerk's forehead creased. "Um. No." His mouth opened, then closed, and a red stain washed up into his cheeks.

Devon hid a grin as Josh turned to her and gripped her upper arm, hustling her over to the furniture arranged in front of the fireplace.

"They're not here," he muttered. "Shit." Then, "What's so funny?"

"I think he thought we were having a little *ménage à trois*. On our wedding night. The poor guy was embarrassed."

Josh stared at her, and then his lips twitched. Well, he still had a sense of humor. That was good, because he was going to need it. Her heart beat a little faster, a rapid percussion against her ribs.

Josh sighed and tipped his head back. "Well. The last ferry's gone. We're stuck here for tonight."

She hadn't thought of that. Of course the last ferry had left. "Well. I'll go...uh..." She had no idea where she was going to go. "Maybe they have another room."

"Are you kidding? This is prime season and it's a weekend. They're booked solid, no doubt. Besides, I've got a suite. There's lots of room for both of us."

She nodded and sank onto one of the chairs facing the

fireplace. Her heart was pounding so fast now she could barely breathe. "It's lovely here," she managed to say, just to make some kind of conversation.

"Yeah."

Allie would have liked it. But Devon didn't say that. The silence grew a little uncomfortable as they waited. God. Mistake. Epic mistake! She nibbled her bottom lip until the man from the hotel approached them, ready to take them to their room.

"Do you need help with your luggage?" he asked.

They both shook their heads, and Josh reached for the key the man held, an old-fashioned, actual key, not a card. "We can find it," he said.

"Second floor," the man said with a smile, nodding toward the wide staircase. "Turn right at the top. It's the room right at the end of the hallway. Call the desk if you need anything at all." His smile widened. "Enjoy your evening."

"Thank you."

They followed his directions, their steps muffled on the beige Berber runner that ran up the stairs and along the quiet hall. On the second floor, more white painted woodwork lined the walls, and sconces cast a warm glow.

Josh unlocked the door, and she followed him into the suite.

"Holy crap," she couldn't stop herself from saying.

Not only was the suite large and luxurious, votive candles flickered everywhere—on the tables in the living room, in the bedroom visible through open French doors, even on the counter in the bathroom. Pink and red rose petals had been scattered over the floor and the puffy white duvet on the bed, and a silver bucket of champagne sat on the console table behind the sofa in the living room.

Josh stopped and looked around, then shoved a hand into his hair. "Shit."

Chapter Five

"I guess we should have told them this isn't really a honeymoon," Devon said, taking in the room.

Josh sighed. "I didn't really want to get into it. I didn't know they were going to do this."

"Well. It's lovely. So romantic."

"Fuck." He watched Devon cross the living room to peer into the bedroom. She turned and surveyed the living room.

"It's a nice hotel," she said finally. She met his eyes, and he caught the faint shadow of sadness on her face. He wasn't sure what that was about. It didn't matter. This was a screwed-up day.

After a short pause, Josh said, "Are you hungry? Everyone else is eating my wedding dinner, apparently, but we didn't get to eat. There are a couple of restaurants in the inn, I think."

"I'm...I suppose I'm a little hungry."

He hauled her suitcase into the bedroom and set it on the luggage rack provided. "You take the bedroom," he said. "I'll sleep out there. I think the couch makes into a bed."

"Are you sure? I can sleep out there."

"No, that's fine."

"Um. Allie might not like us staying in the same room."

He frowned. "Are you kidding? She's the one who left. I could be here with the Kirkland twins and she wouldn't care."

Devon choked on a laugh at his mention of the two sisters in high school who'd allegedly slept with the entire football team, some of them at the same time. "I didn't see them in the church," she said.

He couldn't stop the answering grin that tugged his mouth, and they shared a moment of amusement. He liked it.

"Do I need to change?" she asked. "This seems like a fancy place."

"You're fine." He ran his gaze over her jeans and T-shirt. During the ferry ride she'd slipped on a form-fitting, black zippered jacket. "We'll just go in the bar and have something quick, if that's okay."

"Fine with me. I guess we should blow out the candles." Her wistful look around tugged at something inside him.

"Yeah. They're a fire hazard."

She gave a crooked smile. "Oh right. You would be concerned about that."

With the lingering scent of smoke and melted wax on the air, they left the room and went downstairs to find the bar.

George's Bar was tucked in behind the restaurant, tiny but full of people and chatter, lively on this Saturday evening. They managed to find two seats at the end of the bar. The smiling bartender took their orders for a beer for Josh and a glass of wine for Devon, and Josh picked up a menu. "Fancy stuff," he murmured. He glanced at Devon. "The kind of place you like."

When they'd lived in Boston she'd loved trying out new restaurants. He'd always been agreeable, but his preferences tended toward burgers and simple sandwiches.

She looked over the menu, nodding.

"Seriously," he said. "Why would you ruin perfectly good macaroni and cheese with truffles and kale and caramelized squash?"

She grinned. "They have chicken wings. You like wings. Or you used to, anyway."

"I still like wings. But what the hell, let's be adventurous. How about mussels?"

She gave him a look over the menu. "You think eating mussels is being adventurous? A boy who grew up on the ocean?"

"It's adventurous *here*," he said. "Caramelized fennel, chablis and garlic-herb butter?"

Her lips twitched. "Okay. Let's share those and some hand-cut fries."

"Sure."

A burst of laughter from the group behind them startled him, and he rolled his eyes. He wasn't in the mood to enjoy other people having fun. He scowled at his beer.

His phone buzzed in his pocket again.

"Crap." He pulled it out to check the call display, then shoved it back into his pocket. "My mom."

"Aren't you going to tell her you didn't find Allie?"

"I'll tell her. Tomorrow." He took a big swallow of the fizzy, bitter liquid. Then guilt nudged him. His mom was probably worried sick about Allie. She'd been so invested in this wedding, so thrilled that he and Allie were getting married, that Allie would be another daughter for her and she would get to be the mom Allie had lost.

He also felt guilty about Allie. Should he have tried harder to stop her? Gavin Montgomery wasn't a serial killer, but he'd been trouble back in the day, and he'd hurt Allie before. He should have tried a little harder to intervene.

Wait. He was the one who'd been left at the altar. Why was he feeling guilty? Jesus.

He slanted a glance at Devon. She leaned on the bar like he did, her long chestnut hair hanging down her back, her feet in flip-flops tucked around the rungs of the stool. Despite her casual clothes, she looked classy and elegant.

"What?" she said, turning her head to meet his eyes.

He shook his head. "I'm just confused, I guess."

"Josh." Her eyes softened. "Maybe things will still work out. Maybe Allie will realize she's made a mistake and come back."

He pursed his lips. "Maybe."

Devon looked down at the paper cocktail napkin she held in her fingers. "Would you take her back? If she comes home and says she's sorry, she screwed up...would you take her back?"

He tipped his head back and looked up at the tin-paneled ceiling in the bar. Would he?

There were a lot of good reasons for them to get married. They were good friends and they cared about each other. They shared common goals and values—family was important to both of them. Their families had been intertwined their whole lives, and this would just make it official. His mom loved Allie. His mom had been devastated by the death of Allie's mom last year. She still hadn't really recovered from that, but with the impending wedding, she'd been happier than Josh had seen her in ages. Judging from her repeated phone calls, she still wanted the marriage to take place.

"I don't know," he finally said. He drank his beer again and glanced at Devon. Once again, he caught a flicker of something in her eyes.

"So you might."

He shrugged. "I suppose."

"Really?" She tipped her head to one side.

"I don't know," he snapped, then rubbed his forehead.

"Why do you think Gavin did that?" she asked. "Coming all that way and interrupting the wedding...wow. That takes guts."

"You sound like you admire him."

"Well. You do have to admire someone who goes after what they want."

"Not like that!" He stared at her. "And Allie... Christ." He shook his head.

"You're angry at her."

"Of course I'm angry!"

She nodded but didn't meet his eyes.

Their food arrived and they began to eat. He hadn't really thought he was hungry, but the mussels were really good, perfectly cooked and full of flavor. The fries were freshly cut potatoes cooked to a golden crisp. Between the two of them, they devoured everything.

"Pretty good," he admitted, wiping his fingers on a paper napkin. "For a fancy place. You still like stuff like that? Trying out new restaurants?"

She looked down at her wine glass. "Sure."

"That wasn't very enthusiastic. I thought you loved living in Boston."

"I do. Of course I do."

"How's your job going?"

She didn't immediately answer, then said, "It's fine." She hitched a shoulder. "You know. Same old."

He blinked. Devon loved her job and had had all kinds of ambitions for moving up in the company. She'd loved to talk about it, and he'd always enjoyed listening to her, sounding so smart and passionate. "I heard that you moved."

"Yeah." She'd lived in a tiny little bachelor apartment when they'd been together. "I found a really nice apartment downtown. In a high rise. I like it."

"Big enough to hold your shoe collection?" He'd always teased her about her weakness for shoes.

She gave him a halfhearted smile. "Yes, it has lots of closet space."

"You looked really pretty," he said, surprising even himself with that one. "At the wedding. That was a nice dress."

Her bottom lip pushed out a little, but she still smiled. "Thanks. I didn't get to wear it for very long."

"You'll be able to wear it again."

"True. And that is really the *least* important reason in the world for being sad about what happened today."

He sighed again. "God, Dev. I can't believe it."

"Maybe you should try to call Allie again."

"I've tried. She's either screening my call or has the phone off. Or the battery's dead. She always forgets to charge her phone."

"D'you...think she still cares about him?"

Josh drained his beer while he thought that over. "I don't know. I thought she cared about me." He gave a short laugh. "Obviously I was wrong about that." He knew that Allie had been crazy in love with Gavin at one time, though. And you didn't always get over feelings like that so easily.

He glanced again at the woman beside him, the woman he'd been thinking about the night before his wedding. The woman he still thought about a lot, if he was being perfectly honest with himself. He'd been bitter for a long time after he'd moved back to Promise Harbor, hurt that Devon hadn't been willing to give up big-city life and move back there with him. No, you didn't get over feelings like that so easily.

How differently would things have turned out if she'd come with him? Maybe the wedding today would have been *their* wedding. Christ. That thought just made his gut hurt, so he shoved it ruthlessly away. There was no point in going there. Things were the way they were, and that was that.

"Let's go," he said abruptly, sliding off the stool. He'd signed the bill to have it charged to their room, and he tossed some bills onto the bar for a tip.

Chapter Six

Devon grabbed her purse and followed Josh out of the noisy little bar with an envious glance at a martini a girl was drinking. She needed more than one glass of wine to be able to deal with all this. She wanted to stop and grab that martini out of the girl's hand and toss it back.

As she walked through the small bar, she again scanned the faces of other people there. She hadn't spotted anyone who looked like William Mudge when they'd arrived, either in the lobby or here in the bar. Although all she had to go on was a small head shot from the company website.

But if he was here with his family, he probably wouldn't be in the bar on a Saturday night.

The lobby glowed with low light from the table lamps and the fireplace, outside now totally dark. Josh strode past the chairs and tables and headed up the stairs, and she trailed along behind him. So they were going back to the room. Er, suite. Great.

It was only about nine thirty, a little early for going to bed.

Bed.

She gulped at the thought of being with Josh in a room with a bed.

But she wouldn't. The bedroom was hers, and he was sleeping in the living room. On the couch. That made into a bed.

Really, she hadn't thought this through when she'd suggested this little trip. Her first thought had been holy crap,

Greenbush Island. William Mudge. The real reason she'd come home to Promise Harbor.

Well, mostly.

She hadn't thought past what would happen when they got there and either found Allie and Gavin or not.

Okay, it wasn't a hotel room, it was a *suite*. Lots of room.

When they'd walked in earlier and she'd seen the romantic ambience created by all the candles and flower petals and champagne—oh hey, they could still drink the champagne—she'd found herself on the verge of tears. It was so beautiful and romantic and special. But not for her. It had been meant for Allie, and her heart had squeezed painfully at that realization.

Josh unlocked the door and walked in, and she headed straight for the silver bucket still sitting on the console table behind the sofa. She pulled the dripping bottle out of the bucket and held it up. "No sense in wasting this," she said. "It's a very nice champagne. Let's have some."

Josh threw himself down onto the soft, cream upholstered couch piled with cushions. "Sure," he said. "I don't know anything about champagne." He extended a hand, and she gave him the bottle to open. She picked up the two flute glasses and rounded the couch to sit beside him.

He popped the cork expertly for a guy who knew nothing about champagne, and carefully poured the bubbly golden liquid into the glasses. He reached behind him to return the bottle to the ice bucket, then lifted his glass. "Cheers," he said with a glum smile.

"Cheers." She touched the rim of her glass to his with a gentle clink, then sipped the wine. "Very nice."

Josh picked up the remote control for the flat screen television mounted to the wall above the fireplace, both flanked by feathery palm trees in wicker baskets. Curious, Devon rose and approached the fireplace...yes, it was gas, and she found the switch to turn it on.

"It's fake," Josh said, sounding mildly disgusted.

"It's not fake. It's gas." She returned and sat beside him again, tucking one foot under her so she was at an angle facing him. "You're a firefighter. You should know that's real fire."

He grinned. "You know what I meant. I much prefer a wood-burning fireplace."

"This is nice. And obviously much more practical for a hotel. Safer too, I would think." She gave him a look from beneath her eyelashes, and he laughed.

"Yeah. Safer."

He started clicking through channels on the television. "Maybe we can watch a movie," he said. "No chick flicks about weddings, though."

"Darn. That is *so* what I want to watch right now."

He slanted her an amused glance as he channel surfed.

"You're clicking too fast," she complained. "How can you even tell what the show is when you go that fast?"

"I can tell," he said. "I'm a guy. It's how we roll."

She relaxed a little into the cushions, smiling. The champagne was delicious and cold and had her blood warming in her veins a little.

"*Austin Powers*," he said, pausing. "Yeah baby. That's what we need. Something funny."

"Oh Jeebus Crust."

She'd always laughingly disapproved of *Austin Powers*, and he probably thought that's why she complained, but really she cursed because of the memories it brought back. They'd watched all the *Austin Powers* movies together. She'd loved to tease him about watching something so lowbrow, pretending she was above that, and yet she'd sat there with him and laughed along with him at all the ridiculous penis and bodily function jokes. Then she'd teased him because he'd watched the movies so many times, he knew what line came next at any given moment.

"*The Spy Who Shagged Me*," she murmured.

He held out a fist. "Good job, Dev," he said. "I'm proud of you." She grinned and made a fist and bumped his knuckles with hers. Shaking her head, she dragged her gaze away from Josh's handsome face to look at the big television. She closed her eyes briefly at the emotion that washed over her, a sense of familiarity, of comfort, a rush of warm affection. God. Her heart banged in her chest, and she focused on breathing to slow it down, pretending to watch the movie while her thoughts and emotions rampaged inside her.

He probably didn't expect to be spending his wedding night watching *Austin Powers*.

But she kept that thought to herself, sipping champagne and trying not to cry, until the movie eventually did make her laugh out loud.

Josh glanced at her with a sly smile. "See. You do think it's funny."

They'd had this discussion many times, always with good-natured teasing, often ending with him grabbing her and wrestling her down until she admitted that stupid movies made her laugh, and then he'd kiss her and...

Heat swept from her chest up to her hairline.

"It's ridiculous," she said, tossing her hair back, but she couldn't help but smile.

"I know," he agreed, settling deeper into the cushions. "That's why I like it."

She reached for the bottle and topped up their glasses. After a second glass of champagne, the movie was even funnier, Josh was even cuter, and the whole wedding-interrupted thing seemed like a pesky annoyance. Champagne was good.

When that move ended, *Goldmember* began. "It's an *Austin Powers* marathon," she said with a giggle.

"Lucky us." Then Josh let out a huge belch.

She stared at him in mock horror.

"Excuse me," he said, grinning. "It's the bubbly."

"That was very rude," she said primly. She turned her attention back to the TV. It only took her a few seconds to work up an almost equally impressive burp.

"Good one," Josh said, still grinning.

And she burst into giggles, her head falling back into the couch cushions, tension easing out of her body. Ah god. Laughing was so good.

They watched the next movie too, and somehow she was sitting shoulder to shoulder with Josh, leaning into him when she laughed at the jokes, and then he looked down at her and met her eyes. Awareness of his big muscles made her tingle everywhere, and the air around them suddenly seemed electric. His smile faded, and they stared at each other as moments accumulated and her insides grew heavy and achy. She was close enough to see the whiskers starting to shade his jaw, his long eyelashes, the tiny mole in front of his left sideburn that she remembered so well. She tried to breathe but her lungs were constricted.

Tempting. So tempting, to reach out and touch his face. To kiss his mouth and see if it felt the same, to see if he tasted as good, if he was still the best kisser she'd ever been with. To give in to the emotion welling up inside her, the lust and need and yearning. She'd missed him so much. Maybe he'd missed her a little too...

No. He'd been going to get married. To Allie.

It took everything she had to drag her gaze away from him and look back at the television, trying to shift a little away from him so they weren't touching, without being obvious about it.

74

And once more her awareness was all on the man beside her and not the movie, the jokes going unnoticed as she valiantly fought the attraction that tugged at her, the intense, physical need for him. Jeebus.

By the end of the movie, the champagne bottle was empty and upside down in the ice bucket. Her eyes were getting heavy, and she had to keep herself from resting her head on his shoulder and giving in to the urge to sleep.

"Hey," he said, nudging her, and she jumped. The movie was over. "Tired?"

"Um. Yeah." She blinked. "I better go to bed."

"Yeah. Come on." He held out a hand and pulled her up off the couch. "I wonder if this bed is made up." He yanked off the cushions, then frowned. "Hell. I thought this was a sofa bed."

"It's not?" She peered down blearily. "Nope. It's not."

"Ah well. I'll just grab a pillow from the bed in the other room. Hopefully there's an extra blanket around somewhere."

"You're going to sleep on that couch?" She eyed it doubtfully. "It's way too short for you. I'll sleep there, Josh. I'm shorter than you."

"No. You take the bed."

She sighed. This was where she was supposed to offer to share the bed. It was king size, room for both of them. They could easily sleep there without ever touching. She'd read so many romance novels where this happened, but in romance novels, sharing that bed always led to sex. And the way she'd been feeling earlier, she didn't have much faith in her own abilities to resist him if they climbed into that bed together, no matter how much space was between them.

"Fine," she said, ignoring the guilt that bumped inside her at the uncomfortable sleep he was going to have. Not her problem. She'd have that king-size bed with the beautiful, poufy duvet all to herself.

She washed her face and changed into her pajamas in the bathroom, admiring the luxury of marble floor and counters, the huge Jacuzzi tub with separate, glassed-in shower stall, the thick towels. She emerged to see the lights out in the living room, Josh standing there in the firelight, tossing a pillow and blanket on to the couch, naked except for a pair of snug boxer briefs.

Her stomach dropped and she hesitated, her heart bumping in her chest, her girl parts giving a warm squeeze. Oh Jeebus Crust, son of Gosh. She'd seen him naked many, many times, but holy hell, he was beautiful in the lamplight streaming through the bedroom doors. His shoulders were wide, his upper arms thick with rounded muscles, his chest and abs sculpted into mouthwatering ridges. "Um. Good night," she said.

He looked up at her. "G'night, Devon. I...uh...swept the flower petals off the bed."

She swallowed. "Thanks." She turned toward the bedroom.

"Devon?"

She paused, afraid to turn around and look at him in case she totally lost it and charged across the room to jump him and lick him all over. "Yes?"

"Thanks for coming with me. It would've sucked being alone here tonight."

She nodded, her throat tight. But he *was* going to be alone, alone on that couch, and she was going to be all alone in that big bed. "You're welcome," she managed to say, and then she scurried into the bedroom and closed the French doors behind her.

Breathing rapidly, heart fluttering in her chest, she paused there, hands over her mouth.

Oh man. She still wanted him. How wrong was that? Oh man.

"Would you take her back?" she'd asked Josh earlier of Allie. And he'd said, *"Maybe."*

The wedding may be off, but he still loved her.

She dropped her hands and lifted her chin. Okay. Okay. She'd done the right thing, to resist touching him. Kissing him. Sleeping with him. For a moment she'd been tempted to let down her guard, to reveal her feelings. Good thing she hadn't. She could do this. She was there on Greenbush Island, just liked she'd wanted to be, with a beautiful hotel room to stay in at the very same inn where William Mudge was staying. She sort of needed Josh for that. But she didn't need him for anything else. It was all good.

Josh woke up early with the sun hitting his face through the balcony doors. There was the trouble with an ocean-view room. He rolled his cramped body off the couch and slowly stood, lifting his arms over his head to stretch. Christ, he'd have been better off sleeping on the floor.

He scrubbed a hand over his face and wandered to the balcony doors to watch the sun lift above the horizon, casting its warm, golden glow. He leaned his head against the doorjamb for a moment, heaviness spreading through him as he recalled what had happened the day before.

It was all such a mess. Allie leaving with that jerk. Josh still questioned whether he should have tried harder to stop her. But hell, she'd called the guy the night before their wedding. To tell him she loved him! Or something like that. He wasn't entirely clear on what had been said.

Worry gnawed at his insides. Maybe he *should* have asked Hayley to put out an APB or whatever the cops did when someone was abducted. But then he remembered the look on Allie's face, the way she'd snuggled into Gavin's arms. And he had to admit she hadn't been resisting much. At all.

Fuck it, she'd gone with the guy willingly.

He watched a sailboat zip along the ocean, someone out for an early morning cruise, the sun illuminating the brightly colored sail and glinting off the surface of the ocean, which was the color and texture of polished bluestone marble. Beach grass rising up from the pale sand dunes waved in the morning breeze. It was so beautiful it almost hurt his eyes. He sighed and rubbed the back of his neck.

He couldn't help but worry about Allie, like he'd been worried about her for the last year, since her mom had died. Allie's mom's death had been hard for both their families.

He turned away from the window. He'd seen a coffeemaker on the desk in the room. He'd brew up some coffee and then maybe head out for a run. Running was always good stress relief, with the added bonus of keeping his cardiovascular system in shape.

As he poured water into the small coffeemaker, he eyed the closed bedroom doors, the floral-print curtains on the other side of the glass panes blocking his view of the bedroom where Devon lay sleeping.

He'd now been dumped by two women in the last year— Devon and Allie. What was wrong with him?

He must have lost his mind, coming here with Devon. But he'd really meant it when he'd thanked her for coming. Being alone sure as shit would have sucked donkey balls. It was nice having her there. Except having her there was also strangely...disturbing.

After she'd gone into the bedroom, he'd lain there in the dark, thoughts consumed not with his missing bride but with Devon sitting next to him on the couch, the feel of her all soft and warm, the sound of her laughter, her singular scent teasing him. That unforgettable scent of flowers and fruit—jasmine and mandarin and sweet sugar. He remembered braving the Sephora store to buy it for her, along with the expensive, scented body lotion, that store almost scarier to him than any fire he'd ever fought. That scent had immediately brought memories flooding back: hot, erotic memories of him burying his face in her hair, of him kissing his way down her naked body, of her long hair dragging across his belly when she did the same. His body had tightened into arousal and then the guilt had smacked him yet again, this time guilt over thinking of Devon on the night he should have been celebrating his marriage to Allie.

Jesus, no wonder he'd been stood up at the altar—he was such a pig.

He was pissed at Allie. Something was wrong with this picture. In his world things were black or white. Right or wrong. He always tried to do the right thing. He looked after the people he loved. He kept his promises. So yeah, he was pissed at her, pissed at her for calling her ex, pissed at her for thinking about her ex the night before their wedding, and then for breaking her promise to *him* and leaving with Gavin. He had a right to be pissed, dammit.

But he also had an uncomfortable feeling that he wasn't much better than Allie, despite all his righteous indignation.

He changed into athletic shorts and a worn gray PHFD T-shirt, laced up his Nikes and, with one last glance at the bedroom door, headed out for a run. He crossed the lobby, still quiet this early in the morning. Outside, he paused on the wide veranda, this side of the building in shade, the morning air cool and fresh. Pots overflowing with greenery and flowers sat next to white wicker chairs on the wood floor. An older couple sat drinking coffee, and he watched as they leaned closer and smooched each other on the lips.

He turned away and jogged down the wide front steps, returning an hour later mildly out of breath, his heart nicely accelerated, sweat dripping from his forehead. He almost hated to walk through the lobby like that, but there was no other way to get to the room. He took the wide steps two at a time and strode down the hall, letting himself into the room with the key he'd tucked in the pocket in the waistband of his shorts.

Would Devon be awake? He hoped she was, because he wanted to tell her what he'd seen, what a gorgeous day it was, wanted to take her for breakfast...whoa.

His feet halted as he came face-to-face with a naked Devon emerging from the bathroom.

She stood there, then grabbed at the towel that had slipped off her breasts. Her mouth fell open and scarlet washed into her cheeks in a way that was damn cute. Her hair hung down her back, dripping wet, drops of water glistening on her smooth shoulders.

"Jeebus Crust!" she said. "You scared the crap out of me."

He grinned. "Sorry." He determinedly kept his gaze on her face. He wasn't going to look. She had the towel in place now anyway, but wow, a glimpse of her perfect breasts had just made his day so much better.

"Where were you?" she demanded crossly, turning to go into the bedroom.

"I went for a run." He held his arms out at his sides. "Can't you tell? I gather you just had a shower, so it's okay if I jump in there?"

"Go right ahead," she mumbled. "I'll get dressed."

The bathroom smelled like her. Sweet-scented steam lingered in the air and fogged the mirror. He breathed it in, and goddamn if he didn't get hard again. Well, the next best thing to a run for stress relief was a little hand action, and the shower was as good a place as any. He turned on the water and stepped under the spray. He let the water rain down on his face, eyes closed, let it wash away the sweat, then grabbed a tiny bottle of hotel shampoo and dumped some into his hand. He groaned, the drumming of the water hopefully drowning him out, closed his eyes again and let the feeling build, the pressure, the heat, the sizzle up his spine. Yeah. So good. So...damn...good. His body jerked and he made a guttural noise as he came, pleasure rushing through his veins.

He panted a little, still leaning against the wall, his body now lethargic, heart pounding all over again. Okay. That would take the edge off. Now he could face Devon without worrying about jumping her sexy bones.

Not that he was worried about that.

With a towel now wrapped around his hips, he emerged from the bathroom but came to a dead stop when he saw Devon standing there, dressed in a striped cotton skirt and a pink tank top, her hair and make-up done.

"Let's go for breakfast," she said. "I'm starving."

"Ah. Sure. Okay if I get dressed?"

She crossed her arms over her chest, over those sweet breasts he'd gotten such a lovely glimpse of, and frowned at him. "No, just wear the towel." She rolled her eyes. "Just hurry."

"What's the rush—" His cell phone chimed. He looked over where he'd plugged it in to charge, sitting on the desk. Not a call this time, a text message. Not likely from his mom, who barely knew how to operate her cell phone, never mind send a text. He crossed the room, picked up the phone and peered at the screen. Reread the message. "Oh for Chrissakes, what now?"

"What is it?" Now Devon met his eyes, hers full of concern.

"It is my mom again," he said, shaking his head. "She says Greta has disappeared."

Chapter Seven

Devon gaped at him. "Greta? Disappeared?"

"Good god," he muttered. "I better call her back this time."

"Um. Yeah." But cripes, he was still naked with only a white hotel towel fastened around his hips, so low she could see his obliques angling toward his groin, a faint trail of hair leading down from his navel, widening just above the edge of the towel, making her gulp. Her gaze tracked back up over cut abs and powerful pecs, the dusting of dark hair between flat brown nipples. Oh holy cheese and crackers, he was so incredibly masculine and gorgeous. As he punched in the number, he turned his back, which was equally spectacular, all those little muscles and the ridges of his back narrowing down from wide shoulders to his tight ass outlined by the towel. She couldn't help it. She sighed with the pleasure of just looking at him.

"I can't believe she figured out how to send a text," he muttered. "Mom. Hi. What's going on?"

Devon listened to his side of the conversation, trying to fill in the blanks.

"What do you mean disappeared? When? I'm sure she's fine. She's a grown woman... Yeah, but..." A longer pause. Then... "*What?* Are you serious?" Now a really long pause while he listened to his mom. Devon sat up a little straighter. What was going on? "Oh for fu— I can't believe that. When did this happen? And she didn't even say anything?"

Devon bit her lip.

"I'm sure she's fine, Mom, but I'll come home..." He listened again. His face tightened. Another pause. "Are you sure? Because I can be there in... What? Really? Is he okay?" More listening. "I know, I know. I'm worried too." He closed his eyes. "How about I try to get hold of Greta? Well, maybe there's a reason... No, I don't mean she's ignoring you. I have no idea. Either she'll call you or I'll call you back. In a while. I don't know. Okay, bye." He punched the button to end the call and met Devon's eyes. "Jesus," he muttered. "What the fuck is Greta doing now?"

He returned to sit on the couch again, seeming not to care that he was mostly nude. Devon licked her lips and tried not to look where the towel covered his lap.

"What's going on?"

"Well. Greta disappeared last night after the wedding. Ah...that's why Mom was calling me. When she couldn't get hold of me, she called Ryan." Devon nodded at the mention of Greta's husband. "He told her they split up."

"Holy fishsticks. Really?"

"That's what he said." Josh shrugged. "Greta never said anything to either of us. Good god. What is going on in the world right now?" He tipped his head back and looked at the ceiling. "I should go back. Mom's all in a panic about Greta, but she said not to come back. She's got Owen helping her find Greta."

"Allie's dad?"

"Yeah." A frown briefly creased his forehead. "And here I was thinking Greta was there for her, but instead Greta's disappeared too. Goddammit." He shook his head. "And now I'm worried about her too. And Jesus, Owen has problems of his own. Oh man."

"Didn't you tell your mom you were going to call Greta?"

"Oh yeah." He poked at the little buttons on the phone and

held it to his ear. "No answer." His forehead creased and his mouth tightened. "Shit. What if something did happen to her?"

"Try a text message. In case she's screening."

With a roll of his eyes, he thumbed in a message and hit send. He stared at the phone. Devon reached over and gently took it out of his hands. "She might not answer right away," she said softly. "Go get dressed. I'll answer if she calls."

He met her eyes, his thick eyebrows slanted down. He hadn't shaved and his beard was even darker now on his lean cheeks, jaw and upper lip. It was a very sexy look on him. Along with the nudity. But the worry on his face made her want to reach out and lay a palm on his cheek and try to comfort him.

He gave a short nod and stood, nearly losing the towel in the process, which made her heart leap, but he caught it and fastened it on his hips as he walked over to the duffel bag he'd set in the closet. He grabbed some clothes, hesitated, then disappeared into the bedroom to dress.

Devon stared down at the screen of the phone in her hand. *Come on, Greta. Answer the damn text.*

With this new drama, she'd forgotten about her rush to get downstairs and see if she could conveniently run into William Mudge. She sighed.

When Josh emerged, dressed in a pair of knee-length plaid shorts and a navy T-shirt that hugged his broad chest and big biceps, there was still no reply.

"Nothing?" he said, rubbing the towel over his still-damp hair. It stood up in all directions, and he tossed the towel onto a chair.

"Not yet. Let's go get breakfast."

He muttered something that sounded like more cursing. "But if she hasn't called by the time we're done eating, I'm going back."

She bit her upper lip, then nodded. Shit! He couldn't go back before she'd even had a chance to look around and find Mudge.

They elected to eat on the patio at the side of the resort building, seated near a railing at a small table for two. The wicker furniture and hanging baskets of lime-green sweet potato vines and red and purple petunias created a pleasant view all around them, and beyond the railing the lush lawn of the resort stretched smooth and green, morning dew sparkling in the sunshine. Devon looked over the menu and ordered an omelet with baby spinach and Parmesan cheese, while Josh ordered eggs Benedict. He gave the waitress a distracted smile when she poured coffee for them both.

Devon checked out the other hotel guests, examining the face of every man she could see. Nope. No Mudge. Dammit.

And then Josh's phone chimed. He grabbed it and thumbed the scroll bar. "It's her," he said tersely. "She says she's okay."

"Where is she?"

He shook his head and typed in a response. Then he set the phone down on the table and waited. Tapping his fingers on the glass tabletop. "I told her to call me," he said. "And I told her Mom knows about her and Ryan."

When the phone rang, he grabbed it again. "Greta? What the hell is going on?"

Once again Devon found herself listening to half a conversation. She leaned her elbows on the table and picked up her coffee cup with both hands, watching Josh's expressive face as he talked, his wide mouth moving, his eyes flickering.

"You're fucking kidding me," he said. A pause. "What happened, Greta?" He listened. Rubbed his face. "Seriously? I can't believe this. Why didn't you say anything? Yeah. Yeah, I get it. Hell, Greta." After another pause he said, "I thought you were there to look after Mom. Why?" He frowned. "Because of the wedding being off. I'm sure she's upset." He closed his eyes and pinched the bridge of his nose. She could see how hard it was for him to not be there for both Greta and his mom. "Yeah. You're probably right. Where are you, anyway?" He listened again. "Goddammit, Greta. Do I have to come and hunt you down too?" A pause. "Fine. I won't. But..." His tone softened. "Are you really okay? Are you sure you don't want me to come and get you? Or head to Boston to kick Ryan's ass for you?" He smiled. "Okay. Yeah, I'm okay too. Really. I don't know. I really don't, but...whatever." He met Devon's eyes and she gave him a small smile. "Seriously, if you need anything, call me."

Devon's smile widened. He just couldn't help looking after them.

He set down the phone with another long-suffering sigh. "She won't tell me where she is, just that she's okay."

"What about Ryan?"

He shrugged. "She says she'll tell me more some time, but for now, they're done and she's fine."

"Cryptic."

"No shit." Their eyes met across the table. "Now I really feel like I should go back."

"It doesn't sound like there's much you can do. Sounds like she wants to be left alone for now."

"True."

"Your family relies on you a lot Josh, but they'll survive without you for a few days."

Josh considered that. His family couldn't survive without him. Could they?

The last year and some he'd been basically working two jobs. Long shifts at the fire department also meant he often had several days off in a row, which enabled him to put in time at

Brewster Landscaping. After his dad had died, they'd relied on a manager to keep the business going, but with the collapse of the real estate market and the credit crunch, they'd run into some cash flow problems that Josh wasn't entirely sure how to deal with.

He should go home and make sure everyone there was okay. But he had a week's vacation booked from the fire department. His mom had told him not to come back, and Owen was there helping her. Greta didn't want to be found. He had no fucking clue where Gavin and Allie had gone. What was there to go home for?

"What about you?" he asked. "Don't you have to get back to your job?"

Her eyes dropped to the table. "Um. No. I have some time off."

Well then. "Okay," he said slowly. "Let's stay."

After breakfast, she suggested they go for a little walk and explore the hotel. He'd already done that on his run, but he agreed to show her around. "There's a lot to do here," he said, telling her about the things he'd seen. "There are tennis courts and a pool, of course. The beach is gorgeous, and there's a lighthouse up on one of the bluffs. There's a golf course..."

She gave a little chirp of laughter. "I am not golfing! I tried that once."

He grinned. "I remember. You wanted to learn because it's so good for networking. It didn't go so well. But we can rent bikes or go sailing."

"The pool," she said. "I want to see the pool."

"Okay."

Lots of people had already gathered at the pool on this warm June Sunday morning. Devon insisted on slowly walking the perimeter of the pool, almost as if she was studying all the guests.

"Okay, then," she said brightly when they'd done an odd little circle around the pool. "Let's go back into the hotel."

Inside the lobby, she once again took her time, looking around.

"Are you looking for someone?" Josh asked. A thought struck him. "You don't think Allie's here, but staying in a different room, do you?"

She blinked at him, her mouth open. "No." She frowned. "I'm not looking for anyone."

"Huh. Okay. Well, let's rent bicycles and go for a ride."

"Um. We could do that later." Her head swiveled back and forth again.

He narrowed his eyes at her. "What's going on, Dev?"

"Nothing. Let's go walk by the tennis courts."

"Oookay."

They walked by the tennis courts, then past the marina. He caught Devon's faint sigh.

"Is it lunch time yet?" she asked.

"We just had breakfast!"

She made a face. "Must be all the sea air making me hungry. Let's walk by the pool again."

He frowned. "We've seen it. Do you want to go swimming?"

"Well, I...ah...didn't bring a swimsuit."

"Huh. Well, I'd suggest nude sunbathing, but this is a family resort."

Their eyes met. He knew she was thinking the same thing, remembering their trip to Puerto Plata and the time they'd spent around the pool at the resort. Many of the European women at the resort had chosen to go topless, and somehow Josh had convinced her to do the same. His dick got immediately hard at those memories, the sensuality of her lying there on a lounge chair topless, her breasts exposed to the warm sunshine and the view of anyone who chose to look. Most people didn't—it was just accepted as customary—but Josh sure had. He'd gotten really turned on by it. And so had she.

"I think we could find a shop that sells bathing suits," he said, his voice coming out a little husky. "If we're going to stay here, you'll need a bathing suit. Let's go. Then we can have lunch."

They drove into Silverport, and he parked just off the main street, lined with little shops and restaurants. The found a beachwear shop, and she picked out a couple of suits to try on.

"Do I get to see them?" Josh asked as she headed into a dressing room.

"No." She closed the door in his face.

Devon turned to face herself in the mirror in the small dressing room.

What was she doing there again? She had a moment, closing her eyes, clutching the tiny pieces of fabric to her. William Mudge. Heffington International. Deep breath. She could do this.

She opened her eyes. She hadn't bought a new bathing suit in years. She'd forgotten how depressing it was to try on suits in a little dressing room with harsh lights and an unforgiving mirror. She'd grabbed bikinis because one-piece suits emphasized her thighs, but maybe she should have picked out a modest maillot. This black halter top revealed a lot of cleavage, and the tiny bottoms no doubt showed every inch of her cellulite. But it fit. She tried on the floral print one, a bandeau top that surprisingly fit very well. She sighed. Fine. Whatever.

Back out in the store, she said to Josh, "These are fine. I

89

need something to go over them though." Preferably a big muumuu or something concealing. They flipped through a rack of cover-ups, and she pulled out a long black T-shirt that would do.

As she went to pay, Josh added in a bottle of sunscreen. "I'll pay for all of it," he said. "You're here because of me."

"Don't be silly." She pulled out her credit card.

"Oh, don't be so prickly," he said, nudging her aside and handing the clerk his own credit card. "Let me do this."

She fumed a little as she waited for the clerk to complete the transaction and bag up their purchases.

Outside the store, on the brick sidewalk in the sun, Josh reached for her face and turned it toward him. "You haven't changed," he said.

She frowned. "What does that mean?"

"It's not that big a deal for me to buy something for you. It doesn't make you weak. Just accept it and say 'Thanks, Josh'."

She gazed mutinously at him and then let out a breath. He was right, dammit. "Thanks, Josh."

He smiled and brushed his thumb over her bottom lip. Lightning-hot need jolted her right to her core as he smiled at her, heat building between them. Then he turned away.

She gulped for air, her insides warm and shivering. "I'm going to need a few more things," she said. "I only planned to stay a couple of days."

"Okay. Let's see what we can find."

When they passed a lingerie shop, she paused and glanced at him. "I...er...need underwear."

He lifted one eyebrow and glanced at the little boutique. "Go on. I'll walk a bit farther and see what else there is."

She hurried in and grabbed a few pairs of thong panties and quickly tried on a bra. When she emerged back into sunshine, Josh waited, leaning against a lamppost.

"There are a couple of shops you might like," he said. "Just a little farther up."

"I just need some shorts. Maybe a couple of T-shirts or tank tops."

They found a few more things for her. The little stores had some cute clothes that any other time she would have loved to explore, but she didn't want to spend money, and she was anxious to get back to the inn and resume her hunt for William Mudge.

They returned to the hotel, and she caught Josh eyeing her as she swept the lobby with her gaze, then studied everyone in the restaurant as they ate lunch. Frustration mounted in her.

"Swimming pool again?" Josh asked as they climbed the stairs to the second level.

"Yes. Good idea."

They changed into swimsuits, snagged hotel towels and made a beeline for the pool. After scanning the faces of everyone there, she gritted her teeth in frustration, then turned to Josh. "I think I'd rather go to the beach."

His eyebrows slanted down as he stared at her. Then he shook his head. "Okay."

They followed the path from the inn to the beach. With the long dune grasses glistening in the sun and waving gently in the warm breeze, and the soft sand beneath their feet, she inhaled the sea air scented with salt and fish and sunshine. She tried to exhale all her frustration out.

"Where do you want to sit?" Josh asked.

She looked one way, then the other. Naturally on a hot, sunny June Sunday, the beach was covered with towels and semi-naked bodies. It was a crapshoot. "Let's just walk a bit," she suggested.

Josh shrugged and followed her as she turned right. Her feet sank into the soft sand with every step as she scanned the people lying on towels or sitting in beach chairs beneath colorful umbrellas. Kids ran and screamed and laughed, playing in the waves, digging in the sand. Everyone she looked at wore sunglasses.

This was impossible.

She blew out a breath. "Let's just sit here," she said.

She felt Josh's puzzled glance as he dropped their things to the sand and shook out a towel.

Stretched out on the towel on the sand, warmth seeping into her, relaxation started working its way through her body. Cripes, she hadn't realized how tense she'd been. She took off her sunglasses and turned her face to the sun, the light turning the backs of her eyelids bright red.

She sighed. She shouldn't be lying here. She should be roaming the beach searching for Mudge. Or, if not the beach, other places around the hotel. Jeebus, this was impossible. Why had she thought it would be so easy to find him there?

"You okay?" Josh asked.

"Yes." After a short pause, she said, "This is nice."

Josh shifted on his towel beside her, stretched out on his stomach, his chin propped on his hands. He stared at the Atlantic Ocean. "Yeah, it is. I don't get much downtime."

She glanced at him. "You never were one for relaxing much."

"True." He made a face. "But life's been kinda crazy lately."

"What's been crazy? Other than your fiancée jilting you and your sister leaving her husband and running away."

He laughed. "And that was just yesterday. C'mon." He jumped to his feet. "Let's go swim."

Chapter Eight

Devon protested about cold water, but he dragged her in anyway and they splashed around in the ocean. The coolness was what he needed on his overheated body, and he wasn't just hot from the sun. Lying there beside Devon with her dressed in that tiny little black bikini showing off all that smooth skin and those sexy curves was heating him up. He'd wanted to roll over onto her towel, stretch out on top of her, bury his hands in her hair and kiss her into next week.

Yeah, he needed a nice cold dunk in the ocean. And some shrinkage. Because he shouldn't be thinking things like that.

"I'm going in," she said to him, rising up from the water, rivulets streaming down over that amazing body. He gulped.

"Right behind you," he said, diving once more beneath the surface. When he came up for air, he watched her wading through the water, her hips turning with each step, her ass barely covered by the little bikini that tied on each hip. The bottom curves of her cheeks made his hands itch to reach out and touch.

When he joined her back on the sand, his gaze fell on her shoulders. "Hey, you're getting kind of pink. You need some sunscreen." He found the bottle they'd bought earlier and popped it open.

"I'll do it." She reached for it.

"No, I'll do it. You can't get your back." He held it out of her reach. He wasn't sure why. It was going to be torture, touching her like that. But he wanted to touch her, and this was a good excuse.

He squeezed some of the thick lotion into his palm, then motioned to her to turn. She gave him her back, reaching to lift her hair up and hold it out of his way. He rubbed his palms together, then set them on her shoulders. She was slender, her bones small beneath his hands, and he went still for a moment. Then he smoothed the lotion over her shoulders and down her back, slowly distributing it over her skin and massaging it in. Whoa, those were huge knots in her shoulders.

"You're tense," he murmured. "Relax."

She made a little snort as her head dropped forward, drawing his attention to the nape of her neck, so soft and vulnerable, curving gracefully, damp tendrils of hair clinging there. He wanted to kiss that stretch of tender skin. He wanted to sink his teeth in, so gently, and own her there.

Jesus.

He poured more lotion into his hands to do her sides, his fingers dipping into the curve of her waist, and then her hips and her lower back. He let his fingers brush beneath the bikini bottom over the swell of her butt, and her body tightened again.

"Just getting it everywhere," he said softly. The coconut scent filled his head, the sensation of her warm, smooth skin beneath his hands like a drug flowing through his veins. "Okay, turn around again."

"You're *not* doing my front," she snapped, her voice a bit breathy. "I can do that myself."

He grinned. "Damn."

She turned to face him and grabbed the bottle from his towel. Their eyes met. A hot haze surrounded them as they eyed each other. His heart thudded and his lungs locked, making breathing impossible.

"Josh," she whispered.

"Yeah?"

"What...?" Her question trailed off.

"We have to talk about it," he said.

She lowered her chin. "About what?"

"About us."

"There is no us."

"You know what I mean. We've been dancing all around it and talking about everything but. But we're going to have to."

"What's the point?" She broke the eye contact and put some distance between them, focusing on the bottle in her hand. "Things were done between us a long time ago. You were ready to marry someone else. There's nothing to talk about."

He wanted to sigh with frustration. Then his attention was caught by her spreading lotion over her chest, her fingers sweeping over the inner curves of her breasts, then stroking down over her arms. Her skin gleamed in the sun as she worked lotion into each leg, then lay down again, her body all shiny and sexy as hell.

He needed to go back in the ocean. He grabbed the bottle and covered his own body, so much bigger and bulkier and hairier than hers, with the cream, "Do my back?" he asked her, lifting one eyebrow.

She shielded her eyes with one hand and looked at him. "Josh."

He gave her an innocent look. "Please? You don't want me to burn."

"You don't burn," she muttered, rolling to her side and pushing onto her knees again. "You always did tan so easily. Give me that."

He hid his smile as he turned his back to her. He flinched a little as she squeezed cold lotion directly onto his skin, but when she put her hands on his body he went hot again. God, the touch of her hands on him made his insides burn, and he gritted his teeth against the surge of arousal.

At first her hands were brisk and efficient, but gradually her strokes slowed and deepened, as if she too was enjoying the luxurious indulgence of touching him. He wanted to turn and face her, to see the look in her eyes, but he knew if he did she would stop and turn away, hiding from him. So he remained there, letting the pleasure wash over him, until her hands came to rest on his shoulders. Her body was so close behind him he could sense the warmth of her skin, the movements of her choppy breathing, and his body tingled everywhere with exquisite awareness.

Then he lifted a hand and set it on top of hers on his shoulder. For a moment, they just stayed like that, him with his eyes closed and head bent, longing for her to move that final centimeter closer to him that would press her body to his, his skin yearning for that contact, aching for her to slide her arms right around him. He swallowed through a tight throat.

After a long moment thrumming with tension, she moved away.

"There," she said, the word low and husky. "You should be good."

"Thanks." Still without looking at her, he returned to his towel and stretched out on his stomach to hide the erection throbbing in his loose board shorts.

Neither of them spoke for a long time, the sounds of the beach rising and falling around them: the rhythm of the waves rushing onto shore, the cry of seagulls, laughter from nearby children. Josh willed his body to relax. Now he was the tense one, but it was sexual tension, hot and fierce. Christ, he wanted her.

He kept his eyes closed, his cheek against the towel, arms at his sides. He hadn't felt this horny in...a long time. He tried to think back and remember a time he'd been so on edge. And he had to go back quite a while.

He and Allie'd had a pretty good sex life. When they'd started dating, they hadn't rushed into having sex. It wasn't until they'd decided to get married that they'd agreed it was time they slept together. She was pretty and had an attractive body, and it hadn't been a hardship to sleep with her. It had been...nice.

Only now he was realizing "nice" was actually kind of sad. Compared to the sizzle burning its way through his body, the almost desperate need to touch Devon, to feel her, to kiss her, to bury himself inside her—"nice" was nothing.

Memories of being with Devon flooded back. How could he have ever forgotten what sex with her had been like? Now he was acutely, painfully remembering, scenes of sex in their beds, sex in the shower, Christ, sex in her kitchen, playing through his mind like a porn movie.

He had to stop this. Somehow he'd stopped it for the last year. Somehow he'd put that all out of his head when he'd gotten together with Allie, and he'd been happy to have comfortable, nice sex with her, conveniently forgetting the intensity of his physical connection with Devon. Now his body was on fire, and he began to doubt his ability to control himself.

He thought about Greta. About the news that she and Ryan had split up. His little sister. Jesus, she was always in some kind of trouble.

And he thought about his mom. There was a buzz-killer. He loved his mom and would do anything to look after her, but man, marrying Allie...that might've been a bit too much. Already it was getting to be a struggle to work up a good steam of anger at Allie for walking out on their wedding.

He rolled over and glanced at Devon, stretched out on her back, face turned to the sun, eyes closed. "How're you doing?"

he asked, his voice now sounding normal.

She turned her head and opened her eyes. "Okay," she said. "It feels weird, though."

"What do you mean?"

"Just lying here. I feel like I should be jumping up and rushing off somewhere to do something."

Amused, he asked, "Do what?"

"I don't know. Just something. I always feel like I should be doing something."

"You need to learn how to relax."

"I know how to relax."

"Sure. If you say so. That's why you're lying there thinking about what you should be doing, instead of just enjoying it."

She sank her teeth briefly into her bottom lip, and he knew he'd scored.

"Just say when you're ready to go back to the inn," he said.

"Actually I might want to swim again," she said. "It's really hot."

"Yeah." Really, really hot.

So they swam again, this time keeping their distance from each other in the water, no playful dunking or splashing, and again sat on their towels to dry off and warm up in the sun.

"I love the ocean," Devon said on a sigh, staring at the expanse of water.

"Really?"

She glanced at him. "Why do you sound surprised?"

"Because you live in a big city. And the way you talk about your dad and his business, I got the feeling you didn't like the water much."

She blinked at him. "Well. Um. Actually, I guess I didn't realize how much I miss it until I came back this weekend."

He nodded. "I love it too. It's so powerful."

Again she gave him a sideways look. "Yeah. That's a good word. Lots of people say it's beautiful, and it is, but that's not enough to describe it. Powerful is good."

"It's a nurturer of life. It's kind of humbling, really."

"Yeah. That's right."

A feeling of warmth spread inside him at the fact that she shared his thoughts about the ocean. He loved the ocean. He loved living near it, being on it, being in it. He loved looking at it, at the seemingly endless expanse that stretched across the globe, marveling at the immensity of it, the power and strength of it but also the way it was mysterious and unfathomable. How it could change in an instant from serenity to chaos. Beneath the beauty was the ever-present threat and danger that only made it more fascinating. The constant rhythm, the sense that the ocean was a nourisher of life, never failed to amaze him, to calm him, to put things in perspective. It was difficult to imagine that his problems were the worst thing in the world in the face of such boundless magnificence. With the sky arcing blue above him and the water in front of him and Devon sitting beside him, it was hard to feel down.

He leaned over and snagged his cell phone from where he'd stashed it under his T-shirt. He checked the time. "It's getting late," he said. "We should go back and shower before we go out for dinner. I'm getting hungry."

"Mmm. I guess so. This is so nice. It'd be nice to watch the sunset."

"We can come back later if you want."

With her legs bent up and her arms linked around them, she laid one cheek on top of her knees and regarded him.

At her look, he shifted and said, "What?"

She just smiled and shook her head, rising gracefully to her feet. "Nothing. Let's go."

They flicked sand out of their towels and gathered their things. She slid that big T-shirt she'd bought over her head, hiding his view of her half-naked body. Just as well. Now they had to go back to that hotel room, his body still pulsing with lust.

"Wanna go out somewhere to eat?" he asked. "Or stay at the hotel?"

"Let's stay here."

"Okay. It seems like a nice restaurant. We can go out somewhere tomorrow."

They took turns showering, and Josh waited with excruciating awareness of her in the bathroom, naked, picturing her in the shower with water streaming down her body. Wow. Yesterday he'd been aware of her, definitely, but today it was almost overpowering, the way his body reacted to her presence.

Then it was his turn, and goddammit if he didn't find himself reaching for his aching cock again, hand slicked up with soap, and once more rubbing one out in the shower. Jesus.

It took the edge off a little.

When they were both dressed, Devon wearing that striped skirt and tank top again, they headed down to the restaurant on the main floor. They walked in and waited at the hostess station to be seated. With dusk approaching, the lights in the restaurant had been dimmed, and candles flickered on each white-clothed table. Soft jazz music floated above them.

A man approached them, and Josh recognized him as the man who'd looked after them when they'd checked in yesterday. "Ah," he said with a big smile. "The newlyweds. Welcome. We have a nice table for two. Just one moment."

Josh and Devon exchanged an uncomfortable look. Newlyweds. Right. He never had told them differently. As evidenced by the candles and rose petals and champagne. "Sorry," he said with a shrug.

"So you two are newlyweds," a voice behind them said.

They turned to see a man with white hair and a pleasantly wrinkled face. Josh had seen him that morning smooching his wife on the veranda. The man smiled. "On your honeymoon?" he asked.

"Um..."

"Well, good luck," he said. "The first ten years of marriage are the hardest."

"Oh." Devon blinked at him. "How long have you been married?"

Josh expected to hear an answer like *fifty years*.

"Ten years."

Josh rolled his lips in to stop from laughing, and he and Devon shared a glance of amusement.

"But this is my second marriage," the man said. "So I know what I'm talking about when it comes to marriage."

"Oh."

"Remember. Marriage isn't just a word. It's a sentence."

Devon covered her mouth with her hand and Josh bit back another grin.

"But you're just starting out," the man said. "On your honeymoon. Enjoy! A honeymoon should be like a table."

"A table?"

"Four bare legs and no drawers."

Now Devon couldn't hold back her choked laughter.

At that moment, a woman joined the man, slipping her arm into his. "Oh no, dear. What are you telling these people?"

"They're newlyweds," he said, looking down at her with undisguised affection. "I'm giving them advice."

"Oh lord. You and your advice. I was such a fool when I married you," she said.

He patted her hand. "I know, but I was in love and didn't notice it."

The woman just shook her head, as if she'd heard that before, and they smiled at each other. Josh and Devon exchanged another grin.

"I can seat you now." The man from the hotel returned. "Right this way."

They smiled at the couple, and as Josh turned away, the man caught his arm and said to him in a low voice, "Remember these words for when you two are fighting."

Josh smiled and waited.

"'Honey, you're right'."

Josh grinned and clapped the man on the shoulder before turning away.

"That's definitely your best advice," he heard the man's wife say as he walked away.

"Honey, you're right."

Josh grinned all the way to their table. Once sitting there, they both burst out laughing. "Oh my god," Devon said, reaching for her goblet of water. "He should be a comedian."

"No kidding. Didn't have the heart to tell him we're not married."

Their eyes met. Then they both quickly looked away.

Damn.

How the hell was he going to keep his hands off Devon for the next few days?

Chapter Nine

As they ate, Devon studied the diners in the restaurant, again looking for William Mudge, but with the low lighting and intimate ambience, once more this wasn't a place a family with kids would be having dinner. She should have suggested they go to the more casual restaurant where they'd had breakfast. Shiz.

She swallowed another sigh of frustration. She could not stay here with Josh all week, sharing that suite, feeling the way she did. She was so attracted to him, still. Well, probably more than that, if she looked deep inside herself. But for now, she could admit that she was still hot for him, a physical attraction that made her body ache and pulse.

She had to find Mr. Mudge and make that connection. She'd pinned a lot of hope on this, after pretty much exhausting her list of contacts and still coming up empty-handed. She knew the business was tough to get into, and she'd been so lucky to be recruited by her dream company right out of college.

William Mudge seemed like her last chance. But...once she'd found him, she would have no reason to stay. A rock materialized in her stomach.

"What's wrong?"

She looked up at Josh. "Hmm?"

"You seemed awfully far away, and you looked kind of sad. Is anything wrong?"

"No. Of course not." She forced a smile and reached for her goblet of ice water. "We should look at the menu, I guess."

All through dinner, she struggled to act normally, but she was distracted by so many things—distracted by Josh and her feelings for him, by the sense of urgency that gripped her to find William Mudge and do something, by the mixed-up feelings she had about both leaving and staying. Going back to the suite with Josh made her insides twist with excitement and fear. Things had sizzled between them on the beach earlier, and it hadn't been because of the hot sun. Confusion mingled with lust.

She didn't want to linger in the romantic atmosphere of the restaurant after dinner, so she turned down the offer of dessert from the server. Josh insisted again on paying the bill, and she fought down her instinctive refusal to let him because, well, she didn't have a lot of money left, which only made her insides twist up into tighter knots. So she took a deep breath and said, "Thank you for dinner," as Josh signed the credit card slip.

Acutely aware of his fingers on her low back as they walked out of the restaurant, she focused on breathing.

"So, what do you want to do now?" he asked. "Another movie in the room? A drink in the bar? Watching the sunset?"

Jeebus. Her mind was so scrambled she couldn't make a decision. "Yes," she managed to choke out. Josh laughed.

And then she saw him. William Mudge. Sitting on a chair the lobby. And oh hey, he was alone.

She came to an abrupt halt and Josh took a couple more steps before he realized she'd stopped. He turned. "What?"

"Um." Her mind raced. She blinked rapidly. She licked her lips. "Um. You go on up to the room. I'll be up in a minute. I need to...ah..." She cast her eyes around and spotted the small gift shop. "I need to pick up something."

His forehead creased. "Okay." He gave a small shrug and headed toward the stairs.

Devon lifted her chin and drew air into her lungs. She

straightened her shoulders and marched toward William Mudge. He was looking at his phone, apparently scrolling through emails or text messages. Her heart thudded against her ribs as she paused beside his chair.

"Mr. Mudge?"

He looked up at her. "Yes?"

She gave him what she hoped was a professional smile. "Hi! I'm Devon Grant." She held out a hand and he slowly took it. She gripped his firmly and shook it, still smiling. "This is such a coincidence," she said. "I had lunch with Martin Hirsh the other day."

He gave a puzzled smile. "Oh yes."

"He mentioned that Heffington International is looking for an investment banking associate," she said. "I was so excited to hear that. I've been interested in working for your company for some time."

He looked taken aback. "Um. Really."

"Yes." She increased the wattage of her smile. "I have five years of experience with Englun and Seabrook." She reeled off a synopsis of her education and experience. "Working for a boutique agency appeals to me so much. And as I said, I've been interested in working for Heffington International for some time. I was particularly impressed with the work you did for Kenway. I also worked on a similar account and achieved great results. Net sales increased from 8.6 billion dollars to 11.2 billion, a 9 percent compound annual growth rate. Earnings before interest, taxes, depreciation and amortization increased from 2.1 billion to 3.3 billion dollars over the same period, a 13 percent CAGR. Operating margins increased from 21 percent to 27 percent, reflecting profitable top-line growth and better cost management. I'd love an opportunity to talk with you more about what I could do to help your company achieve those kinds of results."

His frown deepened. A little girl appeared at his side, about ten years old, wearing a coral sundress. "Daddy! We're back from our walk."

"Hey, sweetie." Mr. Mudge smiled at the girl, apparently his daughter. He turned his gaze back to Devon. "I'm sorry, Ms...uh..."

"Grant. Devon Grant." She beamed as her heart rate climbed higher.

"I'm on vacation," he said, rising from the chair. The little girl slid her hand into his and gazed up at Devon. "But I can tell you that we've just hired two associates, and I don't anticipate we'll be hiring again in the near future."

"Oh." Disappointment flooded her. "But Martin said—"

"Obviously he wasn't aware of the most recent developments," Mr. Mudge said coolly. "If you're interested in a career with Heffington International, I suggest you send in your résumé. We'll keep it on file."

"I have a résumé with me." She should have thought of that. That's what she should have said first, dammit. "It's just up in my room. I can go get it and leave it with you—"

"I'm on vacation," he said again, emphasizing the last word. "With my family. They get annoyed enough when I try to combine business with family time. I'm not about to conduct an interview while I'm here. You can send your résumé in to our HR department and if openings come up, you'll be considered along with other candidates."

"But I...I didn't want to interview right now," she said, keeping the smile in place and striving for a light tone. "That's not what I meant. I meant, when you're back in Boston I'd love the opportunity to meet and discuss how I might fit in with your company."

"I'm sorry," he said as the girl tugged on his hand. "We don't have any openings at the present time, as I said."

She swallowed, her throat tight and achy, and watched him walk away, smiling down at his daughter as she towed him toward a woman and a boy talking to the concierge.

"But..." The word barely escaped her lips. Heat washed down over her body and up into her cheeks. Her eyes stung and her legs went shaky. She sank down into the chair Mr. Mudge had just vacated and stared blindly at the big fireplace.

Shit.

There went her last chance. She'd blown it. Totally blown it. She should have approached him differently.

Fueled by a sense of urgency and, yes, desperation, she'd barreled in when it was clearly not a good time for him. She should have picked up on the fact that he wasn't open to a business discussion. But she'd needed to get to him so badly, and she'd been so elated when she'd seen him, she'd just kept pushing. She should have backed off and suggested meeting the next morning for coffee, or maybe just suggested a meeting when they were both back in Boston. Maybe if she'd had a résumé with her, that would have made a difference... But how could she carry a résumé around everywhere she went? Her thoughts tangled up in her head, recriminations and disappointment.

She glanced around. The Mudge family had disappeared. She should go up to the room. Except Josh was there, and she wasn't sure if she had the ability to act as though nothing had happened. A feeling of intense pressure built behind her cheekbones and her eyes burned. A tear slipped out and she brushed it angrily away.

Her insides tight and hot, she covered her face with her hands and bent forward. A shaky sigh leaked out of her mouth and she fought the urge to burst into tears. She never cried. Especially in a public place.

Shit, shit, shit.

What was she going to do now?

Her bottom lip pushed out and she tried to press her lips together. She'd figure things out. Somehow. But for a few moments, she couldn't fight the bleak despair that swept over her.

"Devon?"

Her head snapped up at Josh's voice and a light touch on her back. She stared at him and watched his expression change from mild curiosity to frowning concern.

"Hey! What's wrong?" He dropped to a crouch in front of her, taking her hands. "What happened?"

She again tried a painful swallow. She couldn't speak, her throat was so constricted. Another tear leaked out. And another. The anxiety in Josh's expression multiplied.

"What is it, Dev?"

She just shook her head and closed her eyes against the caring and concern she saw on his face, tears now sliding in streams down her cheeks. Jeebus Crust. How embarrassing. She *never* cried.

"Are you okay?"

She nodded, her bottom lip trembling helplessly.

"Do you want to go up to the room?"

She nodded again, and he straightened and helped her stand. He slid an arm around her waist and she turned into him, instinctively seeking comfort and protection from him as he led the way over to the stairs, up them and down the hall to their room.

Once inside, the storm of emotion somehow exploded in her and a sob burst from her lips. She turned away from Josh, again covering her mouth with her hands, her shoulders shaking. She felt his warmth as he came up behind her, felt the strength of his hands as he laid them gently on her shoulders.

"It's okay," he said. "It'll be okay, Dev."

He didn't even know what was wrong, but his words somehow did help calm her a little. Then his hands turned her. She tried to keep her face averted, but he pulled her into his arms and wrapped her up in them, and she pressed her face to his chest. One of his hands rubbed up and down her back in such a tender, calming gesture, but that only made another wave of emotion rise up inside her, and she sobbed again, this time helpless to stop the storm of tears.

He held her and rubbed her and whispered soothing words to her as she cried. He rocked her a little and pressed his cheek to her hair until she was done, exhausted and limp and embarrassed.

"I need some tissues," she mumbled against his damp shirt, lifting a hand to swipe her face.

"Sure." He released her and moved to the bathroom, returning with a handful of tissues he handed her. "Here, sweetheart."

At hearing Josh call her the affectionate name he used to call her when they were together, more sadness swelled inside her and she broke into more sobs. She hated being like this, out of control, showing her emotions, but it seemed like she just couldn't keep it all in any longer.

Josh's eyebrows sloped down and his mouth straightened into an unhappy line as he observed her being so distraught. "Dev, Dev, sweetheart, it's okay. Please tell me what's wrong. I've never seen you like this."

"I know," she sobbed, mopping her face, but more tears streamed. "I'm sorry. God, I'm so sorry."

"Don't apologize," he said, his voice low. "It's okay. I just wish I knew what I can do."

"Nothing."

"Come on. Sit down. Tell me what's wrong." He led her to

109

the couch and picked up the blanket he'd used to sleep with last night. He wrapped her up in it and his arms again, and she couldn't stop herself from snuggling in to his big, warm body. She let out a long, shuddering breath. He waited.

"I lost my job," she finally said in a small voice.

His body tensed against her. "What?"

"I lost my job," she said again.

"I don't get it. Just now? Did they call you or something? On a Sunday night?"

"No." And she actually chuckled a little at his confusion. "It happened a month ago."

He slid a hand between them and nudged her chin up. He looked at her with adorable confusion and worry. "A month ago? Why didn't you say something? Jesus, Dev."

"I-I don't know. It's humiliating. I didn't want you to feel sorry for me." She'd been worried enough about showing up at the wedding as the rejected girlfriend, never mind the rejected, unemployed, loser girlfriend.

"What happened?"

She met his eyes. "The company had to downsize. They decided I was one of the ones who had to go."

He stared at her in stunned surprise. "How can that be?" he said slowly. "You're so good at what you do. They need you."

She lifted one shoulder. "Apparently not."

"Fuck. That is unbelievable." He shook his head, a perplexed crease still between his eyebrows.

"I didn't really want to talk about it," she mumbled. "It's humiliating."

"It's not humiliating. It's their mistake."

One corner of her mouth kicked up. "Sure."

"Tell me about it."

110

She found herself pouring it all out to him, and he listened, shaking his head.

"It doesn't make sense to me," he said. "I know the economy is still shaky and businesses are still making tough decisions. But hell, Dev."

"I know." She sighed, crumpling soggy tissues in her hand. "I know it's a business decision. But still." She swallowed.

"You gave that company everything you had." He frowned. "Long hours. You took all kinds of courses, and did all that networking. You worked your butt off for that company. Unfuckingbelieveable."

"Loyalty doesn't count for much," she said. "I guess I've learned that lesson."

"Okay, but why were you all of a sudden crying about it tonight? Obviously you knew about this all along. I don't get it."

She caught her bottom lip between her teeth and looked down. This was even more humiliating. "Oh. Well. I spent the last month job hunting. I tried everything. There just aren't many jobs out there. I haven't even had one interview. I've done everything I can think of, called everyone I know who might be able to help me. I've even started looking at smaller companies. I talked to a friend last week who told me his company is hiring, but I needed to talk to the HR director. But he's on vacation. Only I found out...he's here."

Josh blinked. "How'd you find that out?"

"I found out before I came here, from the friend I had lunch with. That's why..." she gulped, "...I decided to come to the wedding. So I could come over here to the island and see if I could find him and maybe try to talk to him about a job."

He tipped his head. "Huh." She watched him processing that in his head. "So...when you suggested coming here to look for Allie, you were really thinking about finding this guy?"

"Yes. But it was like killing two birds with one stone. I

111

really thought this might be somewhere Allie would come. I mean, it was a possibility. Right?"

"Right," he said slowly.

Her heart launched into a rapid percussion against her ribs. "I made that impulsive suggestion, but I never thought you'd come with me. And then I didn't really think it all through, about what would happen after we got here, and..." She shrugged. "It hasn't worked out. I found William Mudge tonight. In the lobby. It didn't go so well."

He studied her. "No job?"

She shook her head glumly. "They just hired two people. I was too late. And he was pissed because I interrupted his vacation, so I'm pretty sure I'll never get a job at Heffington International." She bowed her head briefly, then looked up at him. Her vision blurred with tears again. "I felt so desperate. I've never been in a situation like this. I got recruited right out of college. But now things are tough everywhere. And I don't have tons of experience."

"Huh. What...six years?"

"Yeah. That's nothing compared to a lot of other people searching for jobs. And you know how important my career is to me. Plus..." Once more she hesitated. "I haven't been that great about saving, so I don't have much money left to live off."

He gave a dry chuckle. "You do realize the irony of you being an investment banker and not managing your own money?"

"Yeah. It's hilarious." She rolled her eyes. "Believe me, I'm mad at myself about it. I just got caught up in all the...stuff. You know."

"The clothes. The shoes. The dinners."

"My beautiful new apartment." She gave him a crooked smile.

"That's who you've been looking for. When we went to the pool and the beach and...I got the feeling you were looking for someone."

"Yes."

"Wow." He shook his head. "Jesus, Dev. That's shitty. I know how important your career is to you. I know how much you gave them to them, and how much you loved working there."

Enough of this pity party. She couldn't believe she'd broken down and cried in front of Josh and then spilled her guts, all her humiliation and disappointment and frustration. She never did that. She worked up a smile, sat up and straightened her shoulders. "But I'll be okay. Don't worry."

"I know you'll be okay," he said softly. "Because you're smart and educated and hardworking and passionate."

She blinked.

"What?" Then he laughed. "Now *you're* looking like you're surprised I'd compliment you."

Her bottom lip quivered just a bit. "Yeah. I am actually. I seem to remember you calling me something like a coldhearted workaholic. Way back when."

He stared at her. "Really? I said that?" He shook his head.

"Yes. I believe it was during one of the many circular discussions we had about moving back to Promise Harbor and all the reasons you had to do it, and all the reasons you couldn't stay."

"And all the reasons you couldn't come with me," he added. Then he closed his eyes briefly. "I'm sorry. If I said that. I mean, I guess I did say that, but..." He rubbed his forehead, then looked back at her. "What are you going to do now?"

"I don't know." Her mouth twisted a little. "Now that I found him and blew my only chance to connect with him, I don't know what to do next. Go back to Boston, I guess. Keep looking for a job."

"A month isn't really that long," he said. "You have to give it time."

"I suppose."

They sat there looking at each other.

"When's the last time you took a holiday?" he asked.

She thought about that. "I'm not sure," she finally admitted.

"Probably that week we went to the Dominican Republic."

That had been...three years ago. She looked at him up through her eyelashes. "It might be."

"So stay. Keep me company for the rest of the week. Consider it a free holiday."

She let his words sink in. "I should go back. Keep looking."

"You've sent out résumés. Maybe now you just have to wait."

"So you're going to stay all week?"

He shrugged and looked down. "I guess. I've got nothing to go home to. Mom's got Owen helping her find Greta, who doesn't want to be found. I've got a week's holidays booked off."

It was probably a bad, bad idea. But she had nothing much to go home to either. And she found herself saying, "Okay."

Somehow Devon made it through the week without giving in to the overpowering desire to throw herself into Josh's arms. They kept busy with activities. Josh liked to do physical things that exhausted her, things like playing tennis, cycling and swimming, both in the pool and in the ocean. She managed to avoid the golf course, but he went golfing a couple of times while she lay by the pool reading.

On rented bikes, they explored some of the island, including the beautiful bluffs. They sat on the dunes and admired the old lighthouse. Devon took a couple of pictures with her phone. "I wish I had my camera," she said wistfully. "It's so pretty and charming."

"You've been here before," he reminded her, smiling.

"I know. But not for a long time. I kind of forgot how beautiful it is."

They went whale watching, walked on the beach, and explored some of the shops and restaurants and galleries in Silverport.

By Friday, their last day, she was more relaxed than she'd been in years, but also incredibly sexually frustrated. Only by having some leisure time with no pressure or stress, other than the pressure she felt to jump on Josh and ride him like a pony, did she realize what a toll her busy lifestyle had been taking on her. The headaches she'd had nearly constantly had disappeared. She no longer had that aching tightness in her neck and shoulders and upper back. She no longer had that tight feeling in her stomach, although it returned every time she thought about going back to Boston and resuming her job search.

Probably Josh had been right. This vacation had been good for her.

"You pick the restaurant for our last dinner," Josh said to her that evening. After a sweaty game of tennis, they'd gone back to the suite to shower and change. He lounged on the couch, looking at a book of area attractions, opened to the restaurant section. "We haven't tried this place...The Lighthouse."

"Let me see."

She peered over his shoulder at the advertisement. The

photograph looked lovely. "Okay. Sure."

"Wear that dress."

"What dress? Oh." She only had one dress with her, the one she'd worn to the wedding. "I guess I can."

"I didn't bring much to dress up in, so I won't look as good as you," he said, rolling to his feet and stretching.

In the bedroom, she slid the dress over her head until the layers of chiffon floated around her knees. She smoothed it down over her hips and checked her reflection in the mirror. Spending a week in the sun had given her a light tan that made her eyes glow, along with a few freckles on the bridge of her nose, which she now frowned at. The peach color of the dress looked nice with the new tan, though, and the dress left her arms bare and dipped in a low V in front and back. She put on make-up for the first time in days, shadowing her eyes a little and shining up her lips with a peachy gloss, and she spritzed on a little of her favorite perfume.

She felt like she was getting ready for a date.

But that was ridiculous. Over the week, she and Josh had managed to ignore the heat between them. She knew he felt it too. So many moments, their eyes meeting, their hands touching, when the sparks sliding through her veins made her hot and achy.

She'd also managed to avoid *the talk* he'd wanted to have about them.

Now this was their last night there, and she wasn't actually sure why they were fighting it anymore. She'd almost convinced herself that just giving in to it and having one hot night before they went their separate ways yet again might be worth it. There was just one little niggling problem in the back of her mind...

Allie.

With a sigh and one last glance in the mirror, she opened

the bedroom door and stepped out. Josh had changed too, into a pair of black chinos and a white button-down shirt that he left untucked. It fit his body perfectly, the sleeves rolled up on his strong, tanned forearms. When he looked up at her, his mouth opened and his eyes heated.

He blinked. "Wow, Devon," he said slowly. "Um. Nice dress."

"You saw it before."

He didn't say anything, seeming speechless. "Er. Yeah. You look beautiful."

"Thanks. Are we ready to go?"

"Sure."

They drove to the restaurant in mostly silence—not an awkward silence, but the car was certainly full of awareness. "I'm kind of sad to leave tomorrow," Devon said. "It's so beautiful here."

"Yeah."

"The weather's been great. We were really lucky."

"Uh-huh."

Inane chatter.

She was going to be sad to leave Josh.

There. She'd admitted it. Only to herself. No way in hell would those words get dragged out of her.

Josh had called for a reservation, and they were shown to their table right away.

"This is lovely," Devon said, looking around. Located on the second floor of a gray-shingled building, the restaurant's low ceiling created an intimate atmosphere. The walls inside were shingled as well, painted a soft yellow, and windows lined two walls. An antique oak buffet in one corner held glasses and napkins and cutlery, and more antiques were arranged throughout the space.

The hostess seated them at one of the window tables. Outside, tree branches tossed in the wind that had picked up late that afternoon. Through the other window they could see the ocean, now gray and choppy, the sky low with heavy clouds that were making it prematurely dark. Inside felt cozy and warm, though.

She glanced at Josh as they both looked over their menus.

"Order a nice bottle of wine," Josh said. "Since it's our last night here. You pick something. I don't know anything about wine."

Devon studied the wine list. She'd never known anything about wine, either, growing up, and when she'd started her job at Englun and Seabrook, she'd taken a series of wine appreciation courses so she could appear knowledgeable at business dinners. She spotted a wine she'd had before and liked, but it was sixty dollars. She looked at Josh through her eyelashes. "I don't suppose you'd let me pay for the wine?" she said.

He lowered his menu. "That expensive, huh?"

She grinned.

"You don't need to pay for the wine," he replied with a faint frown. "I know I'm just a lowly firefighter, but I have money. I can afford a nice bottle of wine."

Her mouth dropped open. "A lowly firefighter? Are you freakin' kidding me?"

They faced each other across the table. "I know what I did was never good enough for how you wanted your life to be," he said quietly.

Her jaw dropped. That was just so stupendously wrong, she couldn't even speak. She tried to find words. "That is the stupidest thing I've ever heard you say," she finally managed.

He frowned.

"How could you think that?" she demanded in a low voice, mindful of the hushed atmosphere in the small restaurant. She leaned closer. "That is ridiculous."

"Can I assist you with a wine choice?" The server appeared at their table.

Devon looked down at the menu again, lost for a few seconds, unable to focus. Did he really think that she thought he wasn't good enough? Her eyes burned.

"Um, no," she finally said. She skipped the expensive wine and randomly selected a bottle of Sangiovese from Italy that was half the price.

"Excellent choice," he said. "I'll be back in a moment."

"It's okay, Devon," Josh said, also leaning forward. "I'm not being critical of you. We all want different things from life. So how much did I just spend on a bottle of wine?"

"I didn't order the expensive one."

His eyebrows drew together again. "You could have."

She shook her head. "No. It's not important."

"I know you like nice wines."

"You think you know a lot about me," she said quietly. "It's not really fitting with how I see myself. And I'm not sure who's wrong." She lifted her gaze to meet his eyes.

For a long, drawn-out moment they looked at each other as if transfixed.

The server returned with the wine, uncorked it, let Devon taste it and then poured it into glasses. "Do you need a few more minutes with the menu?" he asked.

She glanced at him. "Yes. Please." They'd barely looked at the dinner menu.

She tried to focus on food, but her skin felt like it was burning, her thoughts scrambled. The menu was mostly seafood with a French influence. She didn't know what to have.

She didn't care. Eventually she settled on the yellowtail sole amandine and closed her menu.

When she'd ordered her sole and Josh had ordered his steak au poivre and they were again alone, she said, "I thought we knew each other so well."

"Devon. We did."

She shook her head, still feeling pinched by his comments. "Apparently not. I never knew you thought that. And I still don't know why."

"Is this when we're going to do it?" he asked. "This is when we're finally going to talk about things?"

Her bottom lip tried to push out, and she sank her teeth into it. "You're the one who wanted to talk."

"It's not that I really want to," he muttered, pushing a hand into his thick hair and looking away. "I just think maybe...we need to." He looked back at her. "All week long I've been feeling like..." He paused, and her mind raced to finish his thought. Was he feeling something between them too? Her heart started thudding as she regarded him across the table. "Like things aren't really finished between us," he finally said.

She lifted her wineglass to take a sip, hoping her hand didn't tremble. She nodded.

"Let's do this later," he said, meeting her eyes. "When we're back at the hotel. For now, let's just enjoy our last dinner."

Again she nodded, trying to figure out what he meant. When he said things weren't finished between them...what did that mean? Did he want more? Did she? Oh god. And then wanting to enjoy their *last* dinner...apparently he *didn't* want more. This was going to be it. And their "talk" was going to be the closure they'd never really had on their relationship.

With a rock in her stomach, she pasted on a smile and talked about the wine, the decor, the weather. They ate their dinner, but she didn't even taste hers, struggling to actually swallow it. When they were offered dessert, they both shook their heads.

"Looks like there might be a storm brewing," Josh commented as they drove back to the inn. Dark clouds gathered out over the ocean, and the wind had picked up, buffeting tree branches back and forth.

"Yes."

Once inside the suite, Josh crossed to the small refrigerator beneath the desk and pulled out another bottle of wine. "I picked this up earlier," he said. "For our last night."

Last night. He'd said it again. It was their last night. Forever.

Cold hands gripped Devon, a feeling of dread and abject fear. It had been so hard losing him last time. Thinking back to her months of utter misery, her insides tightened into painful knots. Now after just this one week together, she was going to lose him again.

But he wasn't even hers to lose. What had possessed her to think she could do this without her feelings for him getting all stirred up again? She shouldn't have come here.

But he'd poured the wine and now handed her a glass. She took it and watched him cross to turn on the fireplace, then sit on the couch, stretching one arm along the back and crossing one ankle over the other knee. He looked at her. Oh. He expected her to sit beside him. Her feet in her high heels felt glued to the floor, her legs stiff. But she managed to somehow walk toward him and sit down. She sipped the wine.

Then she took a deep breath and asked the question that had been burning inside her all evening. "Josh. How could you possibly think I thought you weren't good enough?"

He tilted his head. "I knew the kind of life you wanted. You had your big investment banking career in a big downtown office. You wanted the clothes, the shoes, the dinners in fancy restaurants. I was just a firefighter from a small town who didn't know anything about designer clothes and gourmet food."

"You're a firefighter," she whispered, her throat tight. "You put your life on the line to save other people. You're smart and brave and strong. You were like a...a..." Her throat closed up and she swallowed hard. "You were like a superhero to me. How could you think I thought something like that?" She really, really didn't get it.

His eyes shadowed. "A superhero?"

She looked down, afraid of what he'd see if he looked into her eyes. "Of course," she said. "Jeebus, Josh."

"I'm not a superhero."

She peeked up at him through her eyelashes. He shook his head, his eyebrows slanting down.

"I'm just a guy," he continued. "A guy trying to do the right things. Trying to figure out what the right things are."

Her heart swelled up so big she couldn't breathe. "Tell me. Tell me why you left. Why you came back to Promise Harbor."

"I did tell you, Devon." He rubbed his forehead. "My mom was in bad shape. Allie's family was in rough shape. I had to be here."

She bent her head, so many things coming to mind she wanted to say but couldn't. *I thought they could survive without you. I didn't think you should have to give up the job you loved. I needed you too.*

"My mom went into a depression," Josh continued. "Not just a...funk, or a blue period, or whatever, which would be normal after someone you love dies. She was clinically depressed. I don't know if you've ever seen someone you care about like that, but it's scary."

She met his eyes and watched him talk, watched the emotions cross his face, and her skin went cold.

"The same thing happened when my dad died," he continued, voice low and gruff. "That time, she was worse. She was almost suicidal."

Devon let out a small gasp and lifted her hand to her chest.

"If you can be 'almost' suicidal," he continued grimly. "She talked about doing it, so she obviously thought about it. But she didn't have a real plan to carry it out, and I think it was just the idea of abandoning me and Greta that kept her from doing it." He held her gaze searchingly. "That's why I've always felt like I have to be there for her. When she started going down into another depression, I was terrified, Dev."

"You never told me that before," she whispered.

"I know." He let out a short breath. "I guess I should have. But Mom doesn't like to talk about it, and she never wanted people to know about it. Everyone just thought she was grieving. I really felt like I had to be there."

Devon nodded, her throat aching, pressure building behind her cheekbones. Damn, she was not going to cry.

"And there were problems with the business," he continued. "I keep trying to tell my mom to sell it, but she doesn't want to."

"Why not?"

"I'm not sure. She's never been really involved with it. Maybe she just feels it's a link to Dad. Or she feels some sort of obligation to him to keep it going. But Jesus, I'm lost when it comes to that stuff. And I seem to spend all my spare time working there. Trying to turn things around. Hell, sometimes I even go out and dig up flowerbeds and plant shrubs."

"Do you have trouble finding staff? Is that why you're doing that kind of work?"

"Yeah. We do." He lifted one big, bare shoulder. "Finding skilled staff has always been a challenge."

"What kind of recruitment system do you have?"

He snorted. "We hire anyone with a driver's license, basically. It's not much of a system."

She pursed her lips. "Hmm. Well, that might be part of the problem."

"I know." He sighed.

"I'm not a human resources expert," she said. "But there are different strategies you could try. I assume you advertise in the paper."

"Yeah."

"What about advertising directly to building trades? You'd find people who already have skills."

"Huh."

"For winter when you do snow removal, you could look to industries that don't work in that season. Like farmers. Agricultural workers would be looking to pick up winter work."

"True." He turned his head and looked at her. "What else you got?"

She grinned. "There are other places to recruit from. Government job banks."

"Yeah. We do that."

"Craigslist, Kijiji. Take advantage of the way the world has moved online."

"Never thought about that."

"And maybe hire early for the summer. Before your competitors hire. Pay a few extra weeks of salary to get good people."

"Huh. That's a good idea."

"Maybe you just need better management."

Once again he made a face. "That could be. Bill's been around for a long time, but he's not exactly up on cutting edge technology and management techniques. He knows landscaping, for sure. But use the Internet to recruit staff? Ha! But once again...I don't have time to spend looking for someone else, plus it'd be hard to cut him loose."

Now it was Devon's turn to sigh. She wished her employer had felt that kind of loyalty toward her.

Her goal had always been to work for the largest investment bank she could, where there were lots of opportunities for learning and growth, opportunities for advancement, opportunities to earn bigger salaries and bonuses. And look where that had gotten her. Out on her ass without a thought about how it would impact her.

She knew it was business. It wasn't personal. Tough business decisions had to be made for the good of the company. But still...she couldn't help but think that there were businesses out there that cared more for their people. Because even though she was a finance girl, she knew that people were a company's most important asset.

"And besides, we don't need to be spending more money right now."

"Is that another problem? Money?"

"Well." He hesitated, and she sensed his reluctance to admit to the problems the business was having. "It's not that we're not making money. Basically I guess you'd say it's a cash flow problem."

"Ah. Well, that's not unusual these days." She couldn't keep the edge of bitterness from her voice.

"I know. The real estate market collapsing and the credit crunch have really had an impact on us. Our customers are taking longer to pay. The ones who used to pay in thirty days are paying in forty-five days. Some are paying in sixty days. I know why they're doing it, but we're not a big company and we can't afford to wait that long. We have our own expenses to pay."

"Payroll. Rent. Stock. Equipment," she murmured. Now, financial matters were something she could get into.

"Exactly." He eyed her again. "And that's all stuff I don't really know much about." He grimaced. "I don't know much about payroll and accounts receivable and accounts payable. I know I have to figure it all out, but..."

"You're not supposed to know about stuff like that," she said, sensing how lost he felt in the business problems. "You're supposed to know about extrication tools and combustion and...and...the normal concentration of oxygen in ambient air." She'd always been amazed at the kinds of things he had to know and how smart he'd been about the science of firefighting.

His lips twitched. "Yeah."

"What about getting a business loan?"

"Ha. Not so easy these days."

She nodded. "You know, factoring might be a solution for you. I think Brewster Landscaping is big enough."

He frowned. "What's that?"

"It's a form of financing designed to solve cash flow problems created by slow-paying customers."

"No shit."

She smiled. "You use a company that acts as a financial intermediary between your customers and your company. The factoring company advances your company funds using your invoice as collateral. They hold the invoice until it's paid by your customer. In the meantime, you get immediate funds to meet your expenses without having to wait sixty days or whatever for your customers to pay."

"Sounds good. But still...how hard is it to get?"

"Well, it depends on your customers. If you have good customers with good credit, then it's relatively easy. Easier than other forms of credit. It's okay if they pay slowly, as long as they do pay."

"Yeah," he said thoughtfully. "I think our customers are all good for payment."

"And to qualify, you can't have any legal or tax problems."

"We don't."

"Most factoring plans can be set up pretty quickly. Less than two weeks."

"Shit, Devon. Is that for real?"

She laughed, warmth spreading through her body. "Yes." The admiration in his eyes made something expand inside her, a feeling of being needed. A feeling of strength. A feeling that for once, she could help *him*. She drew in a long, slow breath. "I..." She paused, swallowed. "I could help you with that."

He nodded slowly and their eyes met. "That would be...awesome, Dev. Seriously." He paused. "So, see? I had to come back to Promise Harbor. I told you I had to. And it..." He paused as if his throat might be closing up too. "It fucking killed me when you wouldn't come with me, Dev."

The corners of her eyes stung, her lungs seized and her heart thudded painfully against her ribs. "Oh, Josh."

And then somehow she was in his arms, his big, strong arms, and she wasn't sure who was comforting whom as they hugged, her face pressed against his neck. She felt his heartbeat and the warmth of his body through the fabric of his shirt, felt him swallow and felt his ragged breathing.

She fought back the tears, breathing in the scent of him, a warm, masculine scent of spice and musk, her arms around his neck holding on as tightly as she could.

"You're shaking," he whispered, and when his lips brushed over her hair she wasn't sure if she'd imagined it. "It's okay, Dev. It's okay."

The skin of his neck was right there, and she let her own lips touch it in the barest of kisses. But his body tightened. His hand slid into her hair and gripped a fistful of it, firm yet gentle, and he tugged her head back. She bit her lip and looked up at him.

Her heart trembled at the heat and hunger in his eyes. Her stomach swooped, and she gulped a mouthful of air as his eyelids lowered over gleaming eyes and hers responded the same way. Josh gave a rough groan as he bent his head and kissed her, finally, finally, oh god, finally.

His arms tightened around her, one hand holding her head, his body big and solid against hers. She sank into the kiss, his mouth warm and firm, insistent yet tender. He slid his tongue over her bottom lip, then inside her mouth, stroking against hers, and she opened wider for him, tightening her arms around his neck and pulling herself closer still.

Her head went empty and she gave herself up to it, the sensation of her aching breasts pressing against his hard chest, the erotic rhythm of his tongue sliding in and out of her mouth making her melt between her legs. She let out a soft little moan, slid her hand into his hair, running her fingers through the thick, silky strands, and kissed him with everything she had.

Jeebus, this was crazy. Hot, but crazy. Stupid. But hot. She remembered his taste and the feel of his lips as if the last time they'd kissed had been yesterday, and yet it was new, new and scary and exciting. She loved kissing him. He'd always been such a sexy kisser, seducing her and turning her into a puddle of lust with his mouth. She ached down low inside, her womb clenching hard with wanting him.

He slanted his mouth over hers, deepening the kiss even more. A year's worth of yearning went into that kiss, so achingly lovely and sensual. His hand smoothed down her spine, burning her through the sheer fabric of her dress, and heat spiraled through her. Then her insides jumped as his hand moved up over her ribs and covered her breast.

She moaned into his mouth at the feel of his hand cupping here there, squeezing so gently, and her nipples tightened into hard, throbbing points. His fingertips found the edge of the V-neck of the dress, brushed over her skin, and sensation sizzled over her body, every nerve ending tingling.

"Wanna take this dress off you," he murmured, rubbing his nose along the side of hers. "Want you naked. Under me. Around me."

His words made flames leap inside her and excitement twisted in her stomach.

"Wait," she said with a gasp to get air into her straining lungs. She shifted away from him and panted. "Wait, Josh."

He stared at her, his lips parted, his eyes dark and hungry. "What?"

God, oh god, maybe she shouldn't do this. She just wanted his mouth back on hers, his hand on her breast, wanted him naked too, but... "I asked you before, but I have to ask you again. If Allie came back...if she said she made a mistake and still wanted to marry you...would you take her back?"

She held his gaze as they sat there looking at each other.

Chapter Ten

Josh stared at Devon, his mind a blank for a moment, his body pulsing with lust and heat, his heart thundering. Then he almost laughed. He almost wanted to say, Allie who? Because she was *so* the last thing he was thinking of just then. For a moment, he examined that. Should he feel guilty about that? Probably, given that a week ago he'd been ready to marry her. She'd been the one to end it, but it was possible she would discover she'd made a mistake and come running back.

But if he did feel guilty, it was only because he now realized...marrying Allie would have been a huge fucking mistake.

After spending this past week with Devon, he could see that what had been between him and Allie had been only a little more than friendship. They liked each other. Their families were close. So many people were happy about them getting married that it had felt like the right thing to do. But it hadn't been right. It had been so, so wrong.

He closed his eyes briefly at the realization of what a close call that had been. How could he have married Allie when he still had such powerful feelings for Devon? He'd tried to forget her, but now he knew he never really had, and probably never would.

And that just caused a whole new set of problems.

He opened his eyes and fixed his gaze on Devon's face, so beautiful, her shoulders and arms bare in that pretty dress, so feminine and delicate with layers of sheer fabric wrapped around her slender body, her chestnut hair glinting with red in the firelight, her sexy, tilted eyes gazing back at him apprehensively, waiting for him to answer.

"No," he said firmly.

She swallowed. "Are you sure? You had to think about that."

"Yeah." He sighed but held her gaze steadily. "You know when I make a promise to someone, I keep my word." She nodded. "I don't take things like that lightly, especially a promise to marry someone. So yeah, I had to think about it. But that's the truth, Dev. Allie and I will never get back together."

How could he tell her how he was feeling when they'd just reconnected, when she was leaving tomorrow to go back to her life in Boston, when the things that had come between them were all still there? But he could tell her this much.

"Marrying Allie was a mistake," he said slowly. "People were pushing us to do it. It seemed like a good idea." He lifted one shoulder. "I've always cared about Allie. We grew up together, we both went through our family stuff together, we were both...alone. But I can see now it was never going to work. If Allie decides she made a mistake running away with Gavin and still wants to marry me...well, I don't think it will be hard for me to convince her that would be a disaster."

He reached out and touched Devon's face, her cheek velvety soft beneath his rough fingertips. "I still have feelings for you, Devon. Clearly."

She nodded, and though she didn't say it, he knew she was admitting she had feelings for him too.

So he pulled her back into his arms, bent his head and found her mouth again with his, to show her the feelings he still had.

She tasted so damn good, so sweet, and when her tongue slid along his, his dick jumped in his pants. He was so full and hard he hurt, and he pulled her right onto his lap, one hand on her hip, the other sliding back into her hair. He loved her hair, long and cool and silky, loved wrapping it around his hands. Her mouth opened wider, inviting him in, and he groaned and went for it, kissing her deep and long, lips sliding, tongues twining.

Her body in his arms felt exquisite and right, soft and warm, her dress riding up on her bare thighs, her legs stretched out sideways on the couch, still wearing those sexy heels. He slid a hand down her back to cup her ass, bringing her closer, but it still wasn't close enough. What he'd said earlier...yeah...naked. Both of them.

The fireplace glowed orange and gold and yellow, the dancing flames casting undulating shadows into the dim room. They didn't need the heat from it—they were creating a lot of their own—but still it was nice to know she wouldn't be cold when he peeled that pretty dress off her body.

His hand bunched the skirt of her dress and slowly, slowly dragged it up over her hip, and then he slid his hand under it and found the sweet, soft curve of her butt. His fingers brushed the string of her thong panties, her warm, resilient flesh filled his palm perfectly and he gave a little squeeze that made her moan. He liked making her moan. He wanted to make her moan all night long.

He kissed the corner of her mouth, her cheek, the sensitive spot in front of her ear. He breathed in her scent, her unique female scent mingled with sexy perfume, hers and hers alone. He tugged on her hair to tilt her head and opened his mouth on the skin of her neck, grazed her with his teeth, licked her with his tongue. Her taste filled his senses and he felt drunk on it, like he was high.

"You and me, Dev," he whispered, his mouth near her ear. She shivered and pressed closer still. "Just you and me. Right now."

"Yes." She turned in to him and they kissed again, endless,

deep kisses full of longing and hunger and sweet, melting pleasure.

The urge to strip her bare, push her to her back and thrust inside her was powerful, and he fought it back. They had all night. This night. One night.

Christ. One night. A stab of pain in his heart stole his breath for a moment.

It wasn't enough. Forever wouldn't be enough.

She was still a part of him. When he'd found her crying in the lobby, he'd been stunned. He honest to god didn't think he'd ever seen Devon cry. Her tears had been like an arrow in his chest, and when she'd confessed about losing her job, and then her attempt to find that guy and convince him to give her a job—Christ, that was so misguided it was heartbreaking. He ached for her, for how distressed she was, but what really got him was how she'd opened up and told him those things. Because even though he'd wondered how well he and Devon had known each other, there was one thing he knew about her with sure and certain knowledge—she did not like to be vulnerable.

Chest aching, he caressed her ass, her hip, her thigh, finding the sensitive crease where leg met hip, teasing there with his fingertips. Her hands began an exploration of their own, trailing over his neck, his shoulders, plucking at the top button of his shirt, then sliding inside over his collarbone. Fire burned beneath his skin, his body taut. Their wordless sounds spoke of need and pleasure.

He untangled his hand from her hair and stroked over her shoulder, pushing the wide strap aside to try to get the bodice off her.

"Zipper," she murmured. "It's on the side." She lifted her arm to give him access, and with a smile he found the little tab and tugged it down.

"There we go." Now he easily pushed the dress down her arms, revealing a lacy peach strapless bra. He had to just stare for a moment at the feminine garment and at the curves swelling in the deep plunge of it. "Jesus," he muttered. "How does that stay up?" It looked as if her breasts were about to spill out, and his blood rushed hotly through his veins.

She gave a sexy smile, linking her hands behind his neck and leaning back a little. That gave him an even better view of her cleavage. "It's a miracle," she said.

He grinned. "I know where you shop. Do your panties match?"

"No. I'm wearing white cotton granny panties."

"Ha." His hand on her ass shifted and once more fingered the tiny strip of fabric on her hip. "Nice try."

She wiggled her hips, which were pressing against his hard-on, and he groaned, spears of need stabbing into his balls. He slipped his hand between her legs, and now she gasped. For a moment, he just cupped her there, letting her heat pulse against his hand. "So soft," he said hoarsely. "Hot and soft."

She stared at him with hazy eyes, her lips parted. Her thighs eased a little farther apart, and she swallowed. He let his middle finger dip into her folds, found the liquid heat, and slid inside her. She gave a sharp intake of air and sank her top teeth into her bottom lip. "Devon," he whispered, a little in awe. "You're so wet."

She gave a jerky nod, still hanging on to his neck.

He played there for a while, fingers sliding over plump folds, in and out of her, then finding her clit, swollen and hard. God, he was going to burst, so much heat and pressure were building up inside him. Incredible.

He couldn't believe how aroused she was, creamy and slick and hot. His tongue longed to taste her, and he swallowed hard. His cock strained to be inside her, and he again fought for control. He found her clit once more, rubbed over it in small circles, and she lifted on his lap, her back arching.

"Oh," she said on a long exhalation. "Oh god." She spread her legs wider yet. "Oh Josh."

Oh yeah. Hell yeah. Holding her with one arm and fingering with the other, he watched the flush spread from her chest up into her face, her eyes closed, her lips parted. Attuned to her response to make sure he was doing it right, hitting the right spot, he reined in his own arousal and took her up. Her body tightened, her hips lifted into his hand, her thighs opening and closing ever so slightly as she neared her release. She made soft little sounds that filled him up, so gratifying. And then she cried out, her body going taut and still. Fuck, yeah.

She slumped against him after that, limp and warm. "Oh my god," she mumbled.

He smiled and stroked her hair, pressing her face against him. But only for a moment, because he was hard and hot. He found the clasp of her bra at her back, flicked it open and tugged it from between them. He kissed her cheek and lifted her off him. "Hang on," he whispered. He stood and stripped off his clothes as fast as he could, then reached for her. He dragged the dress bunched at her waist down over her legs, along with her panties. Now they were both naked, the way he wanted them, and he sat down and pulled her back onto him, arranging her on his lap so she straddled him.

Her breasts were at his face, round and full and perfect. In awe, he studied them, holding her hips. "Sweet Jesus, you're so beautiful," he groaned. He rubbed his face against her curves, felt the rasp of his stubble on her soft skin. Then he closed his eyes, turned his face and found one nipple with his mouth. He closed his lips over the puckered tip and sucked, sensation washing over him at the feel of her in his mouth, fitting perfectly. Sliding his hands up her back, he pulled her closer to him and rubbed his tongue over her nipple. Her body rippled in

135

his hands, and she moaned.

He sucked and nibbled and licked for long moments, then switched to her other breast. Her hands clutched his shoulders, fingers digging in, her gasps of pleasure filling his ears, the sweetest sounds. Giving her pleasure, making her feel so good, that was what it was all about.

"Inside you," he muttered, his throbbing cock begging for attention.

"Yes."

She lifted, and he directed his shaft to her entrance. "Oh Christ," he muttered. "Need a condom."

She whimpered. "Do you have one?"

Fuck, did he? He gave his head a shake, trying to think. "I'm sure I have one somewhere. Let me go look." He kissed her mouth, both of them so aroused and on edge they were quivering. Goddammit. Once more he lifted her off him and gently sat her on the couch. In the bathroom, he blinked at the bright light, then dug through his shaving kit. Oh thank Christ, there were a couple of condoms at the bottom. Almost dizzy with relief, he returned to the living room. The dimness and flickering firelight were a balm to his overloaded senses.

She waited for him, and he held up the small packages. Her sexy smile stole his breath, along with her nude body all golden shadows, her hair gleaming dark red and tangled around her shoulders.

He resumed his sitting position and quickly sheathed up, then held out his hands to Devon, who moved back over him, straddling his thighs. His gaze dropped to the small patch of dark curls between her legs, then lower as she widened her stance and positioned herself to take him. She followed his gaze and looked down where his cock rose up between them. Again he fisted himself and found her entrance, so hot even through the thin latex, and he licked his lips.

"Oh yes," she whispered, lowering herself onto him. "Oh god, Josh." Her body closed around him, tight and warm, inch by inch, as she sank onto his cock. Electricity sizzled over his nerve endings, heat cascading over him at the feel of her softness consuming him.

"You feel so good, baby," he whispered, reaching for her waist. "So damn good."

"So do you."

Then she was there, all the way, sitting on his lap with him filling her. She tightened her inner muscles on him and he almost lost it.

"Easy," he said in a choked voice. "Don't move. Not yet."

She leaned forward to kiss him and their mouths met in that warm connection that hit him straight in the heart. Her hands rubbed over his chest, over his pecs, over his nipples, sending more hot spears of sensation to his groin. "Oh yeah," he murmured against her lips. "So good."

She began to move, slowly, lifting and falling in small strokes, and then she pushed back from him, her hands on his chest again, provoking some kind of primal pleasure inside him that made him want to growl like an animal.

The scent of her feminine arousal rose to his nose, heady and dizzying, and he watched with fascination as his cock appeared, then disappeared inside her again, her plump folds parted to take him in. She pressed a hand to her stomach.

"So deep," she whispered, her eyes half closed. "So deep inside me it almost hurts."

"Don't want to hurt you, baby."

"No, no. It's good. So good." She met his eyes, and something snapped between them, hot and intimate.

"Yeah," he agreed, hands tightening on her body, helping to lift her and lower her. "It is."

Then he couldn't take it anymore. He needed it harder, faster, and he gripped her hips and lifted her off him, then yanked her back down so her ass smacked his lap. She must have sensed his desperation because she picked up the rhythm herself, rising and falling more rapidly, riding him. Fuck!

The drag and pull of her body on his dick nearly had his head exploding. He lifted heavy eyelids and watched her breasts bounce enticingly in front of him, her nipples tight and hard. When she raised her arms to drag her hair back and lift it off her neck, her breasts rose too, and along with the utter bliss on her face, the sight nearly undid him. Something clenched in his chest.

"Fuck," he muttered as her ass smacked his lap again and again. "Dev...I'm close."

She moaned and slid a hand down between her breasts, over her stomach and between her legs. Holy hell. She was going to come again. That was fucking awesome.

Her head fell back and her strokes adjusted to her fingers on herself, but it was enough for him. His vision blurred. "Yeah," he grunted. "Make yourself come, baby. Do it."

She bit her lip, her expression absorbed with the pleasure she was feeling, her fingers rubbing furiously, and then she gave a little wail and rippled around his cock. Her entire body went tight and still, and she fell over him, burying her face in his neck. He wrapped his arms around her, pressed his face into her hair, and used his hips and fucked up into her, hard, his thighs tensing with his impending climax.

Sizzling sensation raced from his balls up his spine and back down again, so fucking intense, and then it washed over him, flooding his senses with unbearable pleasure. He cried out, making unstoppable, guttural noises of pleasure as he came inside her sweet body in wave after wave of orgasm.

He held on to her as if he were drowning, and when he

surfaced again, her mouth was pressed against his neck in a hot, open-mouthed kiss. He dragged air into his lungs, air scented with her singular fragrance mingled with sex, which went straight to his head. "Devon," he whispered. "Christ."

His hand found her hair and tugged to lift her head. He needed to see her face, her eyes. What had they done? What had they done?

She gazed back at him with a soft smile and warm eyes, and he sank into that, overwhelmed and relieved.

"Oh, Josh," she whispered, laying her palm on his cheek. "Oh my god."

"I know." He turned his face and kissed her palm. "I know." He closed his eyes again then, his body still pulsing with heat, her body still clasping him.

And with that, his life had just changed. Good. Bad. Hell if he knew. But nothing would be the same again.

Chapter Eleven

Devon sat there straddling Josh's legs, impaled on his still-hard cock, her chest full of emotion. Her body still vibrated with the powerful orgasm she'd just had, still pulsed around him. When their eyes met, everything else faded away, and like he said, it was just them. She touched his face, bristly with stubbled whiskers, admiring the jut of his cheekbones, the shape of his jaw, the slope of his nose.

It was hard to believe she was there with him, in this beautiful hotel suite, having sex with him after all this time. After all those months of missing him, needing him, aching for him.

"Let's go to bed," he murmured.

She loved the sound of that. "Yes." She wrinkled her nose as she eased off him. Separating from him was not enjoyable. She stood on legs that were surprisingly weak and shook back her hair. Josh rose too.

"I'll just get rid of this," he said, looking down at the condom he was removing. As she moved around him to walk toward the bedroom, he gave her ass a little tap, and she shot him a smile over her shoulder.

She pulled back the covers and slid between the sheets, cool against her overheated skin.

Josh.

She sighed and pressed her face into the pillow. She didn't want to think about tomorrow and leaving or what was going to happen after this. Thoughts like that made her hurt inside. For now, she was there with him and after burning for him all week, they'd finally done it. And Jeebus Crust, it had been hot.

Sex with Josh had always been hot. She'd had other boyfriends before him, but with him she'd learned about her sexuality and explored it fearlessly and eagerly. It had never been the same with anyone else, even when it was good. She smiled into the pillow.

The bed dipped as Josh climbed in with her, his body big and warm. She let herself sink into the voluptuous heat and strength of him as he pulled her up against him and wrapped his arms around her.

"God, Dev," he murmured. "All week, I've wanted to sleep in here with you so bad."

All those nights alone in the big bed made her heart hurt. "Me too," she whispered.

"What were we waiting for?"

She shifted a little to see his face. "This might not be the best idea."

His mouth tightened a little. "Okay. Let's deal with it."

"Um...deal with what?" Her insides knotted.

"Come back to the harbor with me."

She was silent as questions backed up in her brain. *Go back to Promise Harbor? With you? For how long? Why?* "I can't."

"Why not?"

"I just..." Why not? She swallowed. "I..."

"There is no good reason. You have no job to go back to. No reason to rush back to Boston."

"Yes." Her head spun a little. "I guess I could do that. It's just...things are so awkward between me and my dad. And now with Susan."

"Susan?"

"Yeah. His neighbor. And uh...girlfriend. I guess. I don't know. He didn't tell me about her, but when I got there last weekend, I discovered they're in a...um...relationship."

"That's nice."

"That's weird."

He chuckled.

"Seriously! My dad...oh my gosh. I guess it just freaks me out a little."

"Well, sure, that's normal. I'd be freaked out too if my mom started dating."

She sighed. "Yeah, I guess."

"So if you don't want to stay with him, stay with me."

He didn't even hesitate to say it. Oh god. Oh god. She couldn't stop the bubble of hope that expanded inside her, even as she knew that was a crazy idea. "Josh..."

"What?"

"That's crazy." She dropped her gaze to his chin. "I can't do that. Can you imagine what people would say? A week ago you were going to marry Allie."

He groaned. "I don't care what people say."

"Yes, you do."

"Well," he said, rolling her onto her back and moving over her. "Maybe I can convince you this way to come back with me." And he kissed her, holding her head in both his hands.

She melted into the bed, kissing him back, her hands on his lower back, his skin warm and satiny. His weight pressed her into the mattress. Oh yeah. That was pretty damn convincing.

Just you and me.

In that bed, in that quiet, dim hotel room, it was just them. Once again, everything else fell away as she lost herself in him, in the pure rapture growing inside her, in the wonderful pain of him so deep inside her, the agonizing pleasure of being with him like this.

"Devon," he growled. "Damn."

She could only blink her eyes in response, her heart pounding in her ears, that ultimate pleasure just out of reach. With every stroke of his body, with every impact of his pelvis against her, she climbed higher and higher. Flames licked over her body.

"Oh god," she whispered as she climbed higher still, sensation twisting inside her into a hot, hard point of near pain, so exquisite. "Oh god, Josh. Yes."

Their skin dampened, their hearts thudded against each other, her entire body went up in flames, heat and light and power.

"Fuck yeah," Josh groaned. "Oh yeah, Dev. I'm coming too...Christ, there it is..."And he gave a roar as his body went tight and still, his hands fisting in her hair, his face pressed to hers. He pulsed inside her, long, hard beats of pleasure.

They clung to each other, breathing fast, for a while. Devon wasn't sure how long as she drifted on a lethargic cloud of bliss. Maybe she slept a little, but as Josh moved on her, she became aware of her surroundings again, their damp skin sticking together, her hips aching a bit. She shifted too, and he slowly moved off her, again that moment of withdrawal unpleasant, and he disappeared into the bathroom for a moment. She stretched her legs out in the bed, the soft sheets sliding over sensitized skin, and lifted her arms above her head for a full body stretch. Oh wow. That was really all she could muster. Just wow.

Josh clicked out the light they'd left on in the living room and turned off the fireplace, returning to the now dark bedroom just as a flash of lightning illuminated the room. He peered out the window. "Blowing like crazy out there," he said. Thunder rumbled in the distance. "And there's the rain." Big drops splattered against the glass panes.

He turned and climbed back into bed with her, once more wrapping her up in his embrace, and she snuggled into him. "It's nice in here," she murmured.

"Yeah."

He stroked her hair and her back and her hip, and for a while they were silent. She tried to process what had happened and what it all meant, but it was overwhelming. She'd had no idea this was where she'd end up when she'd made the trip home for the wedding. It made her ache, the wanting of him, the wanting of so much more. The futility of the wanting so much more.

He'd asked her to go back to Promise Harbor with him. Her immediate, instinctive response had been no, but now...she didn't want to leave him.

That was so dangerous, that kind of feeling, that kind of thinking. So dangerous because she knew only too well how much it would hurt when things ended again. As they would. Her life was in Boston, and his was here, with his family.

She'd always known his family was important to him, including his "extended family" of the Ralstons. She knew his mom mainly as "Mrs. Brewster", her high school math teacher, and it had always been odd seeing her at Allie's place, seeing a teacher as a normal woman with a family and friends. She hadn't met Josh until a couple of years after his father had died, and although she knew he'd looked after his mom and his sister, she'd never realized how hard that had been for his mom, to the point where she'd been nearly suicidal. He'd never told her that before, and it made her ache for him, for how he'd dealt with that at the age of fifteen, just a boy whose dad had died and who was afraid of losing his mother too. It made her ache for all that was beneath the surface. She'd thought hers

144

was the only family with secrets like that, things that nobody talked about.

He cared about his mom and his sister, and he sacrificed a lot for them. The job he'd loved with the Boston Fire Department. Devon had been hurt and angry when he left, that he'd been willing to give up that and give up her so easily to go back to Promise Harbor, those feelings of abandonment she'd experienced when her mother had left resurfacing so painfully.

He was a good man, though. How could she fault him for doing what he thought was right and best for his family? How could she fault him for caring about them the way he did? His loyalty to family only highlighted how different her own family was, a father who'd shut down and wanted nothing to do with her. Josh was different—he was open and honest and loyal and protective.

"You okay, baby?" Josh whispered. Outside, rain fell in a steady thrum, the wind occasionally splattering it against the windows, thunder growling closer and closer.

"I'm okay."

"Why don't you want to come back to the harbor?" he asked quietly.

She hid her face against his neck and breathed in his scent. "You know my dad and I don't really get along."

"Yeah, I sort of know that. I don't really know why, though. You never talked about your dad much."

"There's not much to talk about." She hesitated, afraid to say it out loud, but she knew she had to. "He just doesn't like me very much." There. She'd admitted it.

He choked. "What? You're fucking kidding me."

"It's true."

"How can you say that?"

There in the darkness with her face hidden and his arms

wrapped around her, she felt safe and secure, and she told him things she never had before. "I think I remind him of my mom. I think he blames me for her leaving. No doubt he blames my mom for leaving me with him and making him raise me all by himself."

His hand moved up and down her back in a warm, soothing movement, and he didn't speak for a moment. "Your dad's a good guy," he finally said. "I mean, I don't know him very well, but lots of people like and respect him."

"He *is* a good guy," she said slowly. "It's just me he has a problem with. After my mom left, he shut down. I always felt like he hated me."

"Oh Christ, no, Devon. He's your father. He has to love you."

She gave her head a little shake, still buried in his neck.

"Of course he does." He rubbed her back again. "Why'd your mom leave? Why would he blame you for that?"

"I don't know if he blames me for her leaving. She left because she wasn't happy in Promise Harbor." She told him the story. "She went back to New York, to her family and her life in the city.

"I don't understand how a mom could leave her child," Josh said quietly.

"Yeah. I always wondered when I was a kid why she didn't take me with her. What I'd done that made her not love me enough to want to take me with her."

Josh went very still against her, so still she wasn't sure he was even breathing. When she lifted her head to look at him, his eyes were squeezed shut, his mouth a tight line.

"Hey," she said, smiling. "It's okay. I'm fine with it."

"Oh, Devon."

This was why she never told people that. She hated being

the object of pity. "I'm fine, Josh," she said. "That was a long time ago."

He gave a short nod. "Yeah." He studied her. "Do you feel the same way about Promise Harbor as your mom did?"

She frowned a little. "No."

"No? You wanted to stay in Boston and live in the city and have your career. You must understand why she wanted to leave."

A feeling of pressure rose in her chest. "I never *hated* Promise Harbor. Not the town itself. I just didn't like the memories. I didn't like the way everyone felt sorry for me."

Josh cleared his throat. "First of all, nobody ever felt sorry for you, Dev. They might have felt sympathy for you because of what your mom did. Sympathy for both you and your dad. Because they liked you and cared about you. Not because you were pathetic. People didn't feel sorry for you that way. I remember my mom talking to Allie about you, and how she thought you were so strong and well-balanced despite what had happened."

She swallowed. "Really?"

"Yeah. If anything, that's how people in town saw you. People respected your dad for being a good father to you, for never badmouthing your mom after she left. It's not easy to be a single parent, and probably even harder for a man to bring up a teenage daughter."

Her throat quivered, her thoughts jumbled. "Yes," she whispered. "That's probably true." Could what Josh was saying be right? That she'd never really been an object of pity or shame? "My dad never talked about my mom, not to anyone, not even to me. But I...I wanted to talk about it. At first, I mean. I wanted to understand. I wanted..."

Hell. She couldn't say it. *I wanted to know that I was loved by someone—if not by the mother who'd abandoned me, then by*

147

the father I'd been left with.

She could understand that people outside their family would have seen the two of them making the best of things and getting on with their lives. Because that was what they'd both wanted people to see. But people didn't see the aching loneliness of a young girl who needed love and affection, who so desperately needed to know that she wasn't the cause of her mother leaving, that someone wanted her and loved her.

"Have you ever thought about trying to find your mom?"

She smiled. "All the time when I was a kid. God, all the time." Her smile went crooked. "But she'd left and obviously didn't care. I tried to mention it to my dad once, and he just snapped at me to forget about it. I never really did, but when I was an adult and I could have just gone to New York to find her, then I didn't want to anymore. I don't want anything to do with her. She's never..." Her throat squeezed and she coughed. "She's never come back or tried to see me, and that tells me enough."

"Fuck," Josh muttered. "If she was here right now I'd... Well, never mind."

Her heart swelled at his anger toward her mom. "It doesn't matter," she said gently. "Once again, it was a long time ago."

"Maybe you should come back and talk to your dad," Josh said. "Maybe that's an even better reason to come back. To sit down and fix things with him."

"That'll never happen. He would never do that. Sitting down and talking? Especially about feelings? Not gonna happen in a million years."

"Huh. Really." He went silent for a moment. "So you really don't hate Promise Harbor?"

"No. I do like it. It's pretty and there are lots of great people. I love how much pride everyone takes in the town and all the community spirit. But I'm done there. I don't have anything there anymore." Once more she hesitated. "My dad and I aren't close. Allie was my best friend, but..."

His body tensed at her unfinished sentence. "I know she talked to you. When we started dating."

"Yes." She kept her face buried.

"She said you were fine with it."

Something inside her swelled up, hot and fast. She almost choked on it, couldn't breathe. He must have felt her tension.

"Dev?"

I wasn't fine with it! I hated you both for that! How could you have done that to me?

"We were done," she managed to say.

"But you and Allie aren't friends anymore. Are you." He said it as a statement, not a question. Because he knew the answer.

Her mouth trembled, more pressure building inside her. "I came to the wedding."

"Yeah. You did. Oh Christ, Dev. I'm sorry."

Anger sizzled through her veins. *You think of everyone else. You look after everyone else. Why didn't you think about what that would do to me? To date my best friend. To marry her.* She shoved at his chest, pushing away from him, tangling herself up in the covers.

He grunted. "What?"

"Don't feel sorry for me," she cried. "I'm fine."

They'd just been so intimate, and she'd felt so close to him. Already she was making herself vulnerable just by sleeping with him again, knowing she was going to get hurt again—she did not want to be an object of pity. She did not want him to know how devastated she'd been when he'd left. She was not going to cry in front of him again. She never cried.

He lunged across the bed and grabbed her. "Devon. Stop.

What's wrong?"

"Nothing's wrong!" She struggled against his strong grip, but he hauled her back up against him.

"Bullshit." And he laughed. He actually laughed. And then she found herself pinned to the mattress with a very big, hot man holding her down. She stared up at him.

"I don't pity you," he said gently. "I'm apologizing for screwing things up so badly. Marrying Allie was a bad idea, for so many reasons. And I'm sorry you two aren't friends anymore."

Her throat clogged up as she gazed at him.

"I don't want you to go back to Boston," he added.

His words tore at something inside her. How could he say things like that? He could he be so honest and brave? How could she say no when he opened up like that?

"And you said you'd help with the business. That factoring thing."

Yes. She had said that. For Josh, when you said you'd do something, you did it. And she wanted to be that person too. She liked the fact that he needed her for something. She liked how that made her feel, for once in her life not pitiful and powerless. Instead she felt needed. Strong.

"Okay," she whispered. "I'll come back with you."

Chapter Twelve

"But just until I get the factoring set up for you," she added. "Maybe a week or two. Then I really have to get back to Boston and start looking for a job again."

Well, hell. But that was better than nothing. Josh was kind of amazed he'd gotten her to agree to come back at all.

His heart squeezed. She thought her father hated her, for Chrissake. That couldn't be. And then when she'd mentioned about how she and Allie used to be friends, her words had ripped a hole in his gut.

He tugged on her hair, gently, to pull her head back so he could kiss her. He didn't know how to make it better for her, other than this way. Showing her. He found her mouth in the darkness, her lips so soft and pouty. Her cheek was hot against his fingertips, and she turned in to him, in to the kiss, shifting her body just a little so they fit together even more perfectly. Her fingers tightened on his shoulder, and he felt her pulling herself closer even though they couldn't really be any closer unless he was inside her.

Again. God, again. He wanted to be inside her again. His dick stirred as blood moved south, her naked body in his arms heating him up all over again, her mouth soft and warm sucking at his, so gently, sucking on his tongue, the kiss getting deeper. He wanted her all over again, even more, his emotions getting all tangled up with the lust. It was all he wanted, her, being with her. He could do her again, do her all night, but...*shit!*

He'd used up the only two condoms he had.

"Mmm. Dev?" He brushed his mouth over hers again.

"Yes?"

"D'you happen to have any condoms?"

Her lips pursed and she drew back a little. He could see her shadowy eyes. "Um. No."

"Damn."

He caught the movement of her lips as she smiled. "I wasn't planning on having sex on this trip."

"I wasn't either." Never mind the fact that it was supposed to have been his honeymoon. Once that was off the table, he sure as hell hadn't planned on having sex. "But I want to. Again."

"Ah." She shifted against him, her breasts soft against his chest. "Well, there are lots of other things we can do."

Excitement raced through his veins. "Oh. Oh yeah."

"Like maybe...sleep."

She kissed him softly, but he felt her smile against his lips. He slid his hand down and gave her butt a little smack.

"Hey!"

"Never mind the 'hey'. You like that too." Trying new things, sexy things, had never been a problem for them. He laid his palm on the firm flesh of her ass again, just how he knew she liked it, and she wriggled enticingly.

"Okay, I didn't mean sleep," she said breathlessly.

"Good. I mean, we *should* get some sleep. At some point."

"Sure."

"But not now." He kissed her again, long and deep, molding his palm to her ass cheek, pulling her against his thickening cock, that buzz of need starting in his groin again. Jesus. "I know what I want to do."

"So...do it."

Her words set him on fire, and he gently pushed her to her back. He leaned over her and kissed her, cupping her breast, filling his palm with firm flesh, her nipple tightening against his hand. He bent to suck the other nipple, loving the feel of pebbled flesh against his tongue, loving the way she melted into him. His hand slid down between her legs, found where she was silky and wet. For him. It made his head spin. And made his cock hard.

He explored her body with his mouth and his hands, kissing sensitive places like the inner curve of her elbow and her waist. He turned her over and drew her hair away to lick the back of her neck and drag his tongue down her spine, down, down to the little hollows just above her ass. He kissed her there, palmed her cheeks, then licked the crease where cheek met thigh. He loved every shiver and ripple of her body, every soft sigh and moan as he touched her. He kissed her butt cheeks, sank his teeth so gently into the firm flesh, ran his nose up the crevice between while his fingers explored her from the back, dipping into liquid heat.

"You have the most gorgeous ass," he murmured with one last little nip.

Then he rolled her to her back again and moved over her, his testicles tight and full, his cock aching. It jutted out in front of him as he straddled her, his knees on either side of her waist. She gazed up at him, her eyes moving from his face to his cock, and when she licked her lips, heat shot through him and he smiled. "Yeah," he said, looking meaningfully at her breasts. "You know what I want to do. And then I want you to suck me."

She gave a tiny nod, wide-eyed, and reached for him. He loved how much she enjoyed this too. He kneed his way a little closer and took her hands. "Here," he whispered. "Push your breasts together for me."

She did so, plumping up the soft curves, and with a groan he lowered himself over her. Jesus, that was so fucking sexy,

153

Kelly Jamieson

her soft skin closing around him. "Oh yeah," he groaned, unable to take his eyes off the sight, her sexy curves fitting around him, her expression avid and aroused as she too watched. The exquisite drag and pull on his throbbing shaft had tension building, heat rushing through his body.

He watched, and then he moved again, higher up her body, took hold of his cock with one hand and her chin with other. "Open," he directed her with a little pressure of his thumb on her chin, and she obeyed, so sweetly another rush of adrenaline powered through him. He traced her lips with the head, then pushed into her mouth. Her eyes widened, then half closed with pleasure, and she made a soft sound in her throat. Wet heat surrounded him as she sucked on him, nearly crossing his eyes, nearly blowing the top of his head off. Her lips tightened on him, and he reached out to touch his fingertips to her hollowed cheek as she sucked. *Jesus. Jesus Christ.* Sensation like electrical shocks ran from his cock to his balls and then up his spine. So hot. So sweet. So tight.

He was careful not to go too deep, loving how she let him do this, how she let him dominate her like this when they both really knew she was the one in charge—*oh yeah, all the way baby.* He watched her face, watched her heavy-lidded eyes flicker, watched the expression of pleasure that glowed there. His hips moved, sliding his shaft in and out of her wet mouth, the head of his cock aching, his balls boiling.

"Oh yeah, baby," he whispered, his ass tightening as pressure built inside him. He controlled his movements, but she sucked him deeper, with a firm pressure that consumed him. "Sweet. So sweet, baby. Just like that."

Her tongue licked over the head, swirled around the ridge, and more sensation ricocheted through his body, a barrage of sparks, hot and sharp, up and down his spine. His muscles bunched, and he watched his thick erection slide in and out between her lips. She reached for him then, her fingers finding

154

his balls, teasing over them with delicate strokes. "Christ!" he shouted, rapture burning through him, moisture popping out on his forehead and chest. He shuddered. "Yes. Tongue it. Suck it. Christ, that's so good, Dev."

His balls were so tight as her fingers played with them. He panted for air, his lungs constricted, the base of his spine aching, and he knew he was close, so close. "Dev," he said hoarsely. "Gonna come..."

She acknowledged him with a flicker of her eyes, but only sucked harder, hungrily, taking him deeper, and when he bumped the back of her throat, he lost it. Light exploded in front of his eyes, every hard pulse of pleasure wrenching his muscles as he emptied himself into her hot little mouth. She sucked on him as he came, sucked every hot jet, sensation burning and twisting inside him. He cried out with the relief of it, the beauty of her taking him like that.

He reached out and cupped her face, his breathing ragged, and she let him slide out of her mouth, his flesh still heavy. "Christ, Devon," he whispered, staring down at her in awe. "Christ."

She gave him a smile, her lips swollen and shiny, her eyes warm and sensual. He remembered again what it had been like between them, how much they'd loved to explore and enjoy each other. He'd never in his life been with another woman who seemed to take so much pleasure from that, and it made his chest clench.

He lowered himself onto her, stretching out, and kissed her, so deep, so hot, pouring himself into it, every feeling and emotion that he couldn't name.

She'd said she'd come back to Promise Harbor with him, so maybe they didn't have to have an all-night sex marathon after all. At the moment, he wasn't up for that anyway. But the way he was around her, it wouldn't be long before he was.

"So hot," he murmured against her mouth. "You are so damn hot."

"Mmm. So are you."

"I need a shower."

"What time is it?"

"I have no idea." He kissed her again. "Come on."

"Where?"

He rolled off her and off the bed, tugging her with him. "To the shower."

"Oh. Oh! Well, all right. If I must."

He grinned, holding her hand as he walked from bedroom to bathroom. "I've been wanting all week to see if we'd both fit in this shower."

She gave a cute little blink at the bright light. "I don't think there's much doubt that we'll both fit. It's a pretty big shower."

"True. I guess that's why I was thinking about showers for two." He cranked on the water, then pushed her up against the bathroom wall and kissed her as they waited for the water to warm. Jesus, he loved kissing her. Couldn't get enough of it.

Something expanded in his chest, something like relief that she was going to stay longer, that this wasn't going to be their last night together. He wasn't sure where they were going with this, but he'd worry about that later.

They stepped into the shower and he slid the glass closed behind them, enclosing them in a cloud of warm steam. Water sprayed down on both of them, and he slid his arms around her wet body and just held and kissed her some more. He turned her so her back was to the water, turned her again so his was, getting them both wet all over. Then he reached for the bottle of body wash on a small shelf. He popped the lid and sniffed it.

"I remember buying this for you," he said.

"Not that bottle. The one you bought ran out a long time

ago." He caught the teasing glint in her eye and once more laid a little spank on her butt. She laughed, her face turned up to him, wet hair streaming down her back, her smile so luminous it took his breath away.

"I always loved the smell," he said. He poured some liquid into his hand, rubbed it against his other hand and then reached for her again. Slick with soap, his hands glided over every curve and dip. "Oh yeah. Nothing sexier than slick, soapy skin." He caressed her breasts, fingers sliding over firm, sleek flesh with ease, her nipples hard and tight. His hands shaped her ribcage, her waist and her hips, then cupped her ass and brought her up against him.

"Sex in the shower?" she murmured, arms twined around his neck.

"I need a little longer this time," he said. "Before I can go again."

"Getting old, huh?"

"You're asking for it, aren't you?"

"Yup. You might have to spank me." And once more their eyes met, hers gleaming with amusement, and he couldn't stop the grin that spread across his face. Fun. They'd always had so much fun together. Until the end, when Allie's mom had been so sick, then when she'd died and everything had fallen apart. Then, not so much fun.

But that was in the past, and this was now. And he was having fun.

They washed each other with slow, soapy hands, exploring and teasing with low laughs and soft sighs, and damned if he didn't get hard again when her hands slid between his legs. He was going to need to sleep for a week after this. She ran her hand down the length of his cock and back up, and heat converged there, rushing through his body to that spot, right there where she touched him. She rubbed her thumb over the head, and he swelled into her palm. He groaned and tipped his head back, water rushing over his face as her hands teased him and rubbed him and played with him until he was teetering on the brink.

Her fingers slipped between his thighs, cupped his balls pulled up so tight against him, and gently squeezed. "Fuck," he muttered, pressure building there.

"Want you to come," she whispered, rubbing her face against his chest. He lifted his head and dragged his eyes open to watch her watching herself stroke him right to paradise. His orgasm roared through him, so fast and hot his legs damn near buckled, and he flattened his hands against the wall of the shower behind him as he finished, coming all over her hand, the water of the shower washing it away. She turned her face up to him, her lips parted, eyes bright with delight.

"Jesus," he gasped.

She smiled a sweet, lazy smile and leaned into him. "My turn."

"Oh baby." He shook his head. "Too bad I can't lift my arms."

She turned her face into his neck and pressed her lips there. "Take your time."

He couldn't help the laugh that rose from his chest, and he reached for her, miraculously able to command his muscles after all. She reached for the bottle of body wash without saying a word. He held out a hand for more, then rubbed it over the little patch of curls, sudsing up. She gave a little moan of appreciation and his fingers dipped lower, into her pouting folds, so soft, so incredibly perfect. He turned her in his arms so her back was pressed to his chest, wrapped one arm around her and found her breast while the other slid down between her legs. She leaned back into him as he played and stroked and rubbed, finding the sensitive nub and concentrating there until she went up on her toes, her back arched and she made sexy little noises in her throat.

He bent his head and found her mouth to kiss her, sucked on her little tongue, swallowed those whimpers of pleasure and enfolded her in both arms to hug her tight.

"Done," he muttered. "I am so done. Need sleep."

"Mmmm. Me too."

They dried each other off with slow, almost drowsy moves. He rubbed her hair in a towel held in both hands, gently, then picked up the hairbrush sitting on the counter and carefully worked it through the damp tangles. Facing the steamy mirror, their eyes met in their reflection, hers dreamy and soft, and for a moment they both went still, gazing at each other. He smiled then, and her mouth curved in response as he pulled the brush one last time through the strands, then tossed it back on the counter.

"Bed," he said.

In the dark they found their way back to the bed and climbed in. The storm had passed over now, with only faint flickers of lightning and distant growls of thunder.

"Now just leave me alone for a while," he said to her, his voice thick. "Geez, woman."

She gave a snort of laughter as she snuggled in against him, fitting her body to his perfectly, arms and legs twined, her softness molding to his hardness. "Okay. I'll try."

Chapter Thirteen

They awoke early enough for more sex, but when they remembered the lack of a condom, Josh said, "Tonight. Come to my place tonight. I have lots of condoms there." He grinned. "Cases of them."

"Really?" Her eyes widened.

"No. But I'll get some."

She laughed.

They went for breakfast, packed up and checked out, and Devon gave a last, wistful look at the charming suite as they left. The weather had turned much cooler, the sky still overcast and dull, the ocean gray and choppy beneath the ferry as they traveled back to the mainland. When they'd disembarked, she found her car. Josh lifted her suitcase into the trunk and slammed the lid down.

She wasn't sure why her insides felt all twisty.

"So you'll come to my place later?" he said.

"I don't know where you live."

"Hell." He shook his head. "Well, it's not hard to find. I bought the Cabot place on the edge of town."

"Oh. Really?"

"Yeah. My plan is to fix it up, but I haven't done much yet. It's half-empty but..." He shrugged. "It's mine."

She nodded. "Okay. I know where that is. I'll come after dinner, I guess. I'll go find Dad." Her stomach tightened. "He'll be surprised to see me back so soon."

He gazed down at her and nodded too, then bent and brushed his mouth over hers. "Okay. See you later."

As she turned he gave her butt a little pat, and she gave him a look over her shoulder that was meant to be censuring, but really, she liked it. That little pat reassured her.

She drove to Dad's place on Cranberry Lane. She'd have to see if Susan was home to get the key again if Dad wasn't there. She didn't expect he would be. More likely he was out on one of the boats with some tourists.

Sure enough, the door was locked, so she headed next door and rang Susan's doorbell. She answered it with wide eyes and then a smile. "Devon! You're back."

Devon returned Susan's smile. "I'm back."

"Um...didn't you go back to Boston?"

"No. Actually, I didn't."

"Oh." Susan blinked.

"Can I get the key to Dad's house again? He's not home."

"Of course. Come in." She held the door for Devon, who stepped inside. She studied Susan's pretty yellow and white kitchen, a vase of daisies sitting in the middle of the round, white kitchen table. Susan retrieved the key from a small rack on one wall. "Your dad's at work."

"I figured. I might go down there and see what's happening." Whoa, where did that come from? She'd worked her high school years at the business and wasn't all that fond of fishing anymore.

"He'd love to see you," Susan said.

Devon gave her a long look.

Susan frowned. "What?"

"He won't love to see me," Devon said quietly. "Let's be real here."

Susan tipped her head to one side, peering at Devon

through her glasses. "Why would you say that? He was so disappointed when you disappeared last weekend."

Devon's mouth fell open a little. "I doubt that."

"Devon. Yes, he was. I know he doesn't show much of what he's feeling, but I could see how disappointed he was when he read your note. And I think he was a little worried, too. There were all these rumors about Allie Ralston being kidnapped from her own wedding, and then Greta Brewster disappeared too, and...so did you. I think it scared him a little."

"He could've phoned me to see if I was okay," Devon muttered, a little freaked out by what Susan was saying.

"Yes. He could've. He should've. I told him to. But he just shrugged and pretended everything was fine."

Pretended everything was fine. Yeah, he was good at that.

"Well." She wasn't sure what to say. Susan was probably imagining things. "Thanks for the key."

"No problem at all."

With wave and a smile, Devon followed the sidewalk again out front, around the picket fence and through the gate of her dad's house. Once again she found herself inside with her suitcase alone. She sighed. Maybe she should have gone to stay with Josh.

But whoa. That was terrifying. And crazy.

Unsure how long she was really going to stay, she didn't unpack, just opened her suitcase and shook out a few things to get some wrinkles out of them. Then she grabbed the house key and her purse and went with that crazy idea to drive down to the wharf and see if Dad was around.

Even though the weather had changed from the hot, sunny skies they'd had all week, it was a Sunday in June, which meant Promise Harbor was hopping with day-trippers, weekenders and seasonal visitors. The population nearly doubled in the summer.

It was hard to find a parking spot near the wharf, and she ended up walking a few blocks, which was no hardship since it wasn't raining anymore. Clouds still hung low in the sky, a hint of moisture in the air, as usual carrying the briny scent of the Atlantic Ocean. The beach wasn't exactly crowded since there was no sun, but a few people strolled along the water, some kids splashing in the shallows. She smiled at people on the wharf, walking, leaning on the wooden railing, sitting on benches, many eating ice cream or sipping coffee.

She bypassed the big main wharf for the smaller one that housed several businesses, Dad's charter boats, the whale-watching charters, the place that rented Jet Skis and Windsurfers. The old planks creaked beneath her feet, and through the cracks she could see the ocean swirling. She'd spent so much time there as a teenager and couldn't wait to get a "real job" working in a nice, clean office, but now it felt strangely comfortable being there in such familiar surroundings, the atmosphere relaxed and casual. So different from the intensity of the finance world in Boston, the rush and crush of living in a big city.

She opened the wooden door of the small building that housed Grant's Charters, the painted picture of a sea captain fading and peeling a little. She stepped inside and closed the door. A teenage boy sat behind the counter, where a glass top covered assorted marine maps and photographs of impressive catches. He looked up with a smile. "Hi."

"Hi. Is...Mr. Grant around?"

"Yeah, he's in the office. I'll get him."

"That's okay. I'll just go back there. I'm his daughter. Devon Grant."

"Oh, hey. Nice to meet you."

She moved to the end of the counter and passed behind it,

then paused at the open door to the small office. She took in the papers and books and maps and magazines strewn on a counter, two old wooden desks and a bookshelf. Her dad lifted his head from the computer he sat in front of at one of the desks. He stared at her. Blinked. His eyes flickered, and his mouth twitched. "Devon."

"Hi, Dad."

He slowly stood, a frown overtaking his face. "What are you doing here?"

Yeah, that was the greeting she wanted to hear. But a fair question, really. "I never went back to Boston. I, um, went to Greenbush Island for a week."

His graying eyebrows still knitted together, he said, "I didn't realize you had vacation time booked. Or that you were planning a trip to the island."

"It wasn't really a holiday." She leaned on the door frame. "I..." She swallowed. "I have something to tell you."

He waited.

"I lost my job."

Once again, his features shifted, but his expression was hard to read. He said nothing for a moment. "What happened?"

She made a face. "Downsizing. I was one of the most junior staff."

After another pause, he gave a nod. "I'm sorry, Devon. I know how much you loved your job."

"Yeah." She looked down as sadness once again swept over her at her loss. But it wasn't as painful as it had been a week ago. "I really did." But she lifted her chin and pasted on a smile and met his eyes. "But I'll find something else. It'll be okay."

"Of course it will. You're a bright girl."

Her mouth opened, then closed. "Thanks. So. I went to the island because I'd...well, it's a long story, but I thought maybe I had a lead on a job. But that didn't work out. I had nothing to rush back to Boston for, so I took a little holiday. And decided to come back here for a while. I'm going to, um, help out with some financial stuff at Brewster Landscaping."

Silence expanded around them as he stared at her. "Brewster Landscaping. How did that come about?"

"Well, that's another long story." She forced a bright smile. "At the wedding, I offered to go to the island to see if Allie had gone there. Because that's where they were going on their honeymoon. I wanted to go there anyway, about that job."

"Uh-huh."

"And..." She cleared her throat. "Josh came with me."

"Josh Brewster."

"Yes."

"And you stayed all week."

She nodded.

"With Josh."

She nodded again.

Dad sat there silently. She had no idea what was going on in his head. No idea.

"Are you two back together, then?"

"No. Well." Cripes, what was she supposed to say to that? *We slept together last night. Actually there wasn't much sleeping involved.* Yeah, not really comfortable talking to Dad about that. "I don't know," she finally said. "I'm going over to his place tonight."

He lifted his eyebrows. "Do you think that's a good idea?" he asked.

No, I'm scared spitless! But anger rose inside her too at her father's disapproval. "It's my life," she said shortly. "He wants me to help arrange some financing for the landscaping business. They're having some cash-flow problems and Josh is

165

having a hard time figuring out what to do about it. I have some ideas."

He nodded slowly. "I see."

"So it's okay if I stay with you again? I'm not sure for how long."

"Don't expect much in the way of fancy meals. And I'm not home much."

His gruff tone gave no indication that he was happy to have her there, as Susan had said. But then, she hadn't expected that. She looked at the computer on the desk where he'd been sitting. "What are you working on?"

He scowled. "Some monthly expenses. But the goddamn spreadsheet thing isn't cooperating."

"Spreadsheet thing?"

"Yeah. You know. Excel."

She pursed her lips and nodded. "Yeah, I know. Actually I'm pretty good with Excel. Want me to look at it?"

He shrugged, but since that wasn't a no, she took a seat at the worn, old desk, the powerful new PC looking out of place there. "So what's the problem?" she murmured, her eyes moving over the columns and rows.

"Here." He pointed. "It's supposed to automatically add up every month." His blunt, calloused finger moved across the screen.

"Okay." She clicked with the mouse. "There's no formula there. That would add it up automatically." She glanced at her dad, not sure how much he knew about Excel. She had a feeling not much.

"Shit," he said. "I must've deleted it by accident."

"Here. I can fix it." She clicked again then tapped on the keyboard. With a final tap of the enter key, the sum appeared in the cell it was supposed to.

"Huh," Dad said. "You did it."

She dragged the formula down so it populated the whole column, figures appearing as she did so. "There you go."

"So easy." He rubbed his face.

"Why are you doing this?" she said, spinning the chair a little to face him. "I thought Hal did the books for you."

"He retired. A few months ago."

"Oh. I didn't know that." Their eyes met, and she sensed the unspoken words between them—if she called more often, she would know. But if *he* called more often, she would know. She also would have known about him and Susan. "Are you going to hire someone else?"

"I haven't had time to look. I've just been trying to figure things out myself. It's my business—I should know how to do the books."

She bit the inside of her lip. He was a fisherman. He knew about boats and the ocean, fish and tackle and bait. "Well sure. Maybe I can help while I'm here."

He turned away. "You don't need to do that."

Her breath hitched. "I know. I don't mind."

He gathered up some papers on the counter and stacked them. Cleared his throat. "Well. If you have time." He glanced out the window. "Here comes Enoch with the *Lucky Promise*."

"That's it for the day?"

"Yep. Time for supper. I...uh...was going to barbecue a hamburger. If that's okay for you."

"Yeah. Fine."

She turned back to the computer and resumed studying the spreadsheet while Dad went to bring the *Lucky Promise* in and help the passengers disembark. She found some mistakes and fixed them, looked at the file folder of invoices and receipts next to the computer. And got to work.

"Okay, Devon," Dad said, returning a short time later. "Time to go."

"Okay." She saved her work and shut down the computer. "I parked over on Larch Street. I'll see you at home."

He nodded without looking at her.

She began the walk to her car. What on earth were they going to talk about all alone over dinner? It had actually been easier when Susan had joined them with her easy chatter. Hey, maybe they could talk about Susan. Or they could talk about themselves. Like Josh had said.

Or they could talk about nuclear physics or existential phenomenology.

Ha.

Making the meal kept them busy. She sliced hamburger buns and found condiments in the fridge while he got the hamburger patties grilling on the barbecue in the back yard. "There's a bag of potato chips in the cupboard," Dad said.

"That's not a very healthy dinner." She meant it to be teasing, but when he frowned, she realized he'd taken it as criticism. She closed her eyes, holding the bag of chips she'd pulled out. "I was kidding, Dad. I love chips."

He shot her a surprised glance.

"I assume you don't eat them every day," she added.

His lips pursed a little. "No. That I don't."

After a few moments of silence, she said, "I got the key from Susan again."

Dad grunted.

"She's really nice."

"I guess."

"You never told me that you were seeing someone."

"Well. You know. It's..."

She studied his face, tanned and square jawed, his eyes so blue, his short hair brushed back from his forehead. "There's no reason you can't have a relationship with a woman."

He pushed back his chair abruptly. "I know."

Do you love her? How can you love her when you couldn't love me? Her chest clenched.

He carried his plate over to the counter, his back to her, and began running water into the sink.

"You should get a dishwasher," she said, rising to carry her plate over as well. She guessed that was it for their father-daughter conversation.

"I don't need a dishwasher for one person."

Great. They couldn't have a conversation about anything without arguing. After she helped him tidy up the kitchen, she picked up her purse. "Okay. I'm not sure what time I'll be home, but I still have Susan's key."

"Fine. Have fun."

But the look he cast her was almost...worried.

Chapter Fourteen

Josh went home first, but he knew he was going to have to go see his mom and make sure she was okay. She'd told him she was fine and was dealing with Greta's disappearance, with the whole wedding-being-off thing and with Greta's marriage ending, but that hadn't completely reassured him.

He dropped off his stuff, then headed over to Mom's place. But to his surprise, she wasn't there. Huh. Where could she be? Saturday afternoon, he supposed she could be out shopping or something. With a shrug, he climbed back into his car and went back home. He'd talk to her later.

Next stop was Allie's place, to check on her dad. Since Owen's accident, he'd had a few cognitive problems, and Allie worried about him. Josh often helped out with things around the Ralston house, things that overwhelmed Allie. Her brothers were there, but they weren't all that responsible, and since Allie had disappeared he'd better make sure Owen was okay.

It wasn't like Allie at all to just abandon her family. Which once again made him worry a little. But hell. She'd been looking after everybody for so long...he couldn't blame her for wanting to disappear.

Huh. He'd come a long way since being pissed off at her for doing that.

But he struck out again at the Ralston home, nobody answering the door, not Owen, neither of Allie's brothers. Well, another call he'd make later.

Back at his place, he opened some windows to let air into

the house that had been sitting closed up for the last week. He looked around, wondering what Devon would think of the place. It was kind of weird, but when he'd bought it, he'd found himself wondering the same thing, thinking that she would like the hardwood floors and the big, carved baseboards, but would hate the tiny kitchen and bathroom. The house was old and needed a lot of work, but that was the only way he'd ever be able to afford a place this size on such a large lot. A full two stories, the colonial-style house had four bedrooms upstairs with a fifth on the main floor, which that he'd already converted to the great room.

Then he and Allie had decided to get married, and he'd turned his mind to thinking that it would be a good home for a family. He and Allie had never really talked about having kids, but he'd assumed they would one day.

His eyes fell on the boxes sitting on the floor of the empty living room. Shit. Allie'd started bringing some of her things over the week before the wedding. And there were more upstairs.

He had to get rid of those.

He took the stairs two at a time and strode into his bedroom. He flung open the closet, a nice, big walk-in he'd carved out of the bedroom next door when he'd knocked down the wall between them. He grabbed Allie's shirts hanging there, a pair of jeans and, goddammit, in one of the drawers of the built-in dresser he found a few pairs of panties. He scooped them up, then spied a pair of flip-flops on the floor. With all her things gathered into his arms, he ran back downstairs to find a big trash bag. He shoved the clothes in, unconcerned whether they'd be wrinkled or not. He returned to the master suite and entered the bathroom. Bottles of Allie's shampoo and conditioner. Her little pink shaver. A hairbrush and a toothbrush and a bottle of some face-wash stuff. He added all that to the bag and swept his gaze over both bathroom and bedroom once more, then nodded.

Back downstairs, he added the bag to the boxes in the corner, but when he returned to the kitchen he spotted a fashion magazine on the counter, and then a hoodie Allie must have left draped over one arm of the chair in the corner of the great room. He got rid of those too and looked around again. That had better be it.

Okay. Good thing he'd noticed that.

He'd have to get that stuff back to Allie at some point. A brief flare of anger reignited at how she'd handled ending things between them. Jesus. He rubbed his forehead. He'd put off thinking about that stuff, but there were wedding gifts they'd have to return. What a mess. Ah well.

He wandered into his kitchen and peered into the fridge and cupboards. Yep, needed food for the coming week. Tomorrow morning at eight he started a twenty-four-hour shift, so he'd better get out and pick up a few things. Maybe a nice bottle of wine to have when Devon came over.

His insides warmed at the thought of seeing her again that night as he scooped up his car keys and once again headed out.

At the grocery store, the first person he ran into was Mrs. Benedeto. "Josh," she said, her face fully of sympathy and curiosity, laying a hand on his arm. "How *are* you?"

Ah hell. While he'd had the last week to get over it and accept that what had happened was for the best, the rest of the town didn't know that.

"I'm fine," he said. "Great."

"Uh-huh." Clearly she didn't believe him. He caught Coby working the nearby checkout watching them with interest. And there was Ethan, one of his coworkers from the fire department, approaching.

"Josh," he said. "How're you doing, buddy? Okay?"

Fuck. He hadn't anticipated this.

"Yeah," he said again. "I'm good."

"Sorry to hear about the wedding," Coby said, and both he and Ethan eyed him sadly.

"Um. Yeah."

"Is Allie back?" Coby asked.

"I have no idea," Josh said. He smiled.

Mrs. Benedeto frowned. "You didn't go after her?"

"Well, I tried." That sounded lame. "I have no idea where they went."

"I thought you would. You're such a good boy."

He resisted the urge to roll his eyes.

"When she was kidnapped like that, we thought you might get the police involved."

Rumors. Great. He could only imagine what people were saying. "She wasn't kidnapped," he said. "She went with Gavin of her own free will."

"That's not what I heard," Coby said.

Josh gritted his teeth.

"You poor boy, you must be so brokenhearted," Mrs. Benedeto said.

"Um. Really, I'm okay. Look, I need to pick up a few things. Nice to see you again." And he separated himself from them to grab a shopping cart and booked it down the produce aisle.

Shit. The whole town was feeling sorry for him. He hadn't really thought about what he was going to say to people. Apparently Allie wasn't back. Maybe he should try to call her.

He whipped out his cell phone, found her in his contacts and punched the button to dial her. But within seconds, he heard, "The cellular customer you have dialed is unavailable".

Okay. Fine. He'd deal with this when he got home, track

down his mom, Greta, Allie, *somebody* who knew what was going on. He started tossing things in his cart, including a package of condoms. Next stop, the liquor store for wine.

Wyatt Schyler who owned the liquor store didn't give him another sorrowful sympathetic look. Instead he looked at him with slitty-eyed hostility. Wyatt was some distant relative of Allie's. "Josh." His eyes flashed. "So you're back to face your shortcomings, I see."

What the fuck? His shortcomings? He frowned. "Uh..."

"How could you do that to Allie?" Wyatt demanded. "That sweet girl. And then abandon your own family. And hers."

"I didn't... What?" Josh rubbed the back of his neck. "Do what to Allie?"

Wyatt shook his head. "If you'd given her the support she needed, she wouldn't have left you. That poor girl."

Josh's eyes nearly popped out of his head, they flew open so wide. Jesus Christ! "I'm the one who got left at the altar!"

"As I said."

What the fuck? Josh shook his head. "I just need a bottle of wine."

"Sure. Maybe this Heartbreaker Cabernet? Or how about the Dirty Scoundrel Chardonnay?"

"Cute." What was it Devon liked? "How about a zinfandel."

Wyatt lifted an eyebrow. "Zin, huh? Ooookay. Got some nice ones from California here."

"Not too cheap."

Wyatt gave him a look over the top of his reading glasses. "Trying to impress a lady?"

Josh ran his tongue over his teeth. "Maybe." Let people talk about *that.*

Wyatt muttered something under his breath that almost sounded like "asshole" and Josh's eyes widened. Then Wyatt said, "How about this Original Sin Zin. Twenty-two ninety-nine. It has nice blackberry aromas with suggestions of red cherries, sweet oak, a touch of caramel and spicy background notes."

"I'll take it." Never mind the goddamn cutesy name and the fancy description. And the price! He whipped out his wallet and smacked some bills on the counter so he could get out of there.

On the way out he bumped into Elfreda Winning.

"Josh!" she said. "There you are, you dear boy. Are you okay?"

"I'm fine," he said through gritted teeth. Christ, what was worse? Feeling like a pathetic loser or being wrongly accused of being an asshole? "How are you? How's your arthritis?"

"My knees are swollen up like basketballs," she said cheerfully. "Otherwise I'm fine."

"Good, good. Nice to see you." He made his escape, dashing directly to his parked vehicle in the small lot. Safely inside, he paused to get a breath, hands clenching the steering wheel. Dammit, what the hell had been going on all week?

As if he hadn't felt guilty enough, although that had dissipated when his mom had insisted he didn't need to come back, guilt now smacked him in the back of the head. He'd been off having fun with Devon—oh man, had they had fun—while the whole town either thought he was off licking his wounds and crying into a beer somewhere, or thought he deserved being left at the altar because he hadn't been...what had Wyatt said...supportive? Holy fucking shit!

He'd just bought food but didn't really feel like cooking. But as he pulled up in front of Prego Pizza, he paused. He was probably going to encounter someone else he knew who either thought he was a pathetic loser or hated his guts. So he changed his mind and drove home instead. He'd heat up a couple of the frozen Pizza Pops he'd just bought.

While the pastries heated, he called his mom. When there

was still no answer at home, he called her cell phone, and hey, she answered.

"Mom," he said. "Where are you?"

"Josh! Did you find Allie?"

He winced. "Er, no. I'm home now. I came by to see you today, but you weren't home. Is everything okay?"

"Everything is fine."

"What about Greta? Where is she?"

"Greta...well, that's a long story."

His mom's voice sounded funny. Softer. "But she's okay?"

"She's actually...fine."

Seriously? Greta, the family screwup, was fine? What was Mom not telling him? "And Allie? Has anyone heard from her?"

"No." Her voice sharpened. "I was hoping you had."

"No." Guilt backed up inside him again. What if Allie wasn't okay? He closed his eyes and pinched the bridge of his nose. "I did try, Mom, but I didn't have any luck, and frankly, I have no idea where they went. I've tried calling her but she's not answering."

To his utter shock, his mother said, "Oh well."

He held out the phone and stared it.

"We've all tried to call her too," she said with a sigh, "and she's not answering any of us. At least you did try. Are you okay, Josh? You must be devastated about this."

He gave his head a little shake. "No, actually, I'm not," he said. "I have to tell you, Mom, this past week made me realize that marrying Allie would have been a very bad idea."

After a pause, she said softly, "Yes. I think you're right."

Holy shit. "Where are you, anyway?" he asked.

"I'm on Greenbush Island."

What? Once again he held the phone away and stared at it.

Then, "Seriously?"

"Yes. With Owen."

Once again he gaped. "Owen? Allie's dad?"

"You know another Owen?"

"Uh. No. But...what are you doing there?" Jesus. Maybe he didn't want to know that.

"We're just having a little vacation."

"Uh. Okay." He gave his head a shake. This was freakin' weird. "Are you two... Never mind." Yeah, he did *not* want to know.

She laughed. "We're fine, Josh. Anyway. I don't know what came over Allie, but there must have been some reason for her to do that. But...rumor has it you weren't alone on Greenbush Island."

His jaw went slack. Man, nothing was secret in this town. "Mom..."

"We'll talk when we're back."

"Uh. Yeah. Okay."

What was up with his mom going off to the island for a vacation? Well, maybe it was good for her. Obviously, she was dealing with Greta's marriage falling apart, and she seemed to be getting over him and Allie splitting up.

He was just cleaning up after eating when he heard a car outside. He headed to the front door and stepped out onto the veranda to watch Devon park in his driveway. Warmth spread through him at the sight of her.

She spotted him at the door and smiled. "Hey." As she climbed the steps to the wide veranda, she looked around at the house and the yard. "This place is huge."

"Yeah. And half-empty. But I got it for a good price because it needs so much work."

She pursed her lips, no doubt taking in the peeling paint

and the loose board on the steps. "It's a great house, though."

"I like it. Come on in." He held the door for her. "I'll give you a tour."

He showed her the front rooms. He wasn't sure what to call them since they had no furniture in them. "I guess this would be the living room and that's the dining room."

She gave him an amused glance. "You weren't kidding when you said half-empty."

He grinned. "I don't need that much space. I mostly live in the kitchen and great room. I've already redone that. Come see." He led her past the staircase and into the kitchen, which was now spacious and bright. "I knocked out the wall between the old kitchen and a bedroom and made it into one big great room."

"Oh, this is nice."

She surveyed maple cabinets and granite countertops, the counter of one long edge of the U-shaped kitchen separating the kitchen from living space with his big, blue leather sectional, a stone fireplace and big-screen television. French doors led out onto a deck overlooking the big backyard.

"Thanks. I planned to do a lot of the work myself, but I haven't had time to do nearly as much as I wanted. I replaced all the windows right away—they were all old and drafty. I had to put in a new energy-efficient furnace and upgrade some plumbing and electrical. You can't really see that stuff so it doesn't look like I've done much yet. But the kitchen had to be the first thing. It was awful."

She ran a hand over a shiny counter. "I love it."

"I bought a bottle of zinfandel," he said, moving to where it sat on the counter.

"Oh. Nice. Are you offering me a glass?"

He grinned. "Yeah, that was the idea." As he removed the

wrap and the cork, he said, "I'm told it has aromas of, um....berries and oak and...spices."

She giggled. "Sounds lovely."

He poured some into two glasses and handed her one. She breathed in the aroma, then took a sip. "Very nice." She peered at the bottle. "Original Sin Zin?"

"Yeah. Hey, Wyatt recommended it. After he tore a strip off me for letting Allie down."

"*What?*" She stared at him.

"Oh yeah. I'll tell you about it in a minute. Let's finish our tour. There's a small bathroom and laundry room down here," he said, showing her. She checked out those rooms, nodding. "Come on upstairs."

The big staircase would be gorgeous one day. He'd already ripped up the ugly carpet runner, leaving bare wood steps, but they needed refinishing like the rest of the hardwood floors. "I want to do the floors," he said. "And strip the paint off this banister. The bedrooms are all nice and big though." He showed her two empty rooms, and then the third. "I redid this too, since I sleep here every night. I turned the smallest bedroom into an attached bathroom."

She stepped into the master suite. The floor hadn't been refinished, but a nice area rug lay on the worn floor, a sage green that matched the duvet cover. He'd painted the walls a softer shade of that green and the woodwork a creamy white. A big chair sat near the window, which also had a window seat. Then she spotted the double-sided fireplace in the wall between bath and bedroom. "Oh wow. A fireplace in the bedroom and the bathroom. But hey...it's a gas fireplace."

He made a face. "It's more practical up here."

"Uh-huh." She shot him a smirk.

She walked over to peek into the bathroom. "Holy fishsticks. This is...decadent."

He laughed. The bathroom was large, with lots of stone tile and a long vanity counter with double sinks. The raised whirlpool tub sat right beside another window that looked out onto the woods behind the house. "Yeah. I'm not one for long bubble baths, so I don't make much use of the tub, but I thought..." He stopped. He'd thought women liked bubble baths, and the last few months he'd been imagining Allie living there with him. "Well, it's nice to have. I like the shower."

"It's beautiful." She turned away from him, but not before he caught the expression on her face, the droop of her mouth and lowered eyelashes.

He didn't know what to say. He hadn't bought the house for Allie. He'd bought it for himself, but the reality was that Allie had been going to move in with him after the wedding. Although she didn't really get why he wanted to buy a fixer-upper and thought he should have bought one of the new homes being built on the other side of town, which would've been much less work.

And since he'd been so busy helping out at the landscaping business, helping his mom take care of her place, relieving Allie when her family stressed her out, *and* doing his firefighting job, that might have been the better idea after all. He repressed a sigh.

"Devon."

She turned to him, a bright smile in place. As always. "What?"

He didn't know what to say. "I encountered some craziness today. How about you?"

Her forehead creased a little. "Just my dad."

He laughed. "Your dad's not crazy."

"I'm not so sure." She sighed. "But what did you encounter?" Holding her wineglass in both hands, she sat on the edge of his bed.

"Everywhere I went, I ran into people who knew about the wedding. Most of them were all 'poor Josh, are you okay?', but then Wyatt at the liquor store was all pissed and said I'd basically deserved to be left at the altar since I hadn't given Allie the support she needed."

Her mouth dropped open. "Seriously?"

"Yeah." He walked over and sat beside her. In his bedroom. On his bed. With Devon. "I guess people have been talking. Oh hell."

"What?"

His mother's comment about the rumor he hadn't been alone suddenly made things a little clearer. "Um. Apparently there's a rumor that I wasn't alone on the island. I, ah...don't know if people know it was you."

"Oh." She bit her lip. "Well. You know what this town is like."

"I know. Believe me, I know. I mean, usually it doesn't bother me. I just accept it. I love living here, and hey, it's a small town, what do you expect? But today...well, they either thought I was a big loser or a big asshole."

"You're not a loser."

He arched a brow, and she burst out laughing. "Or an asshole. And I'm sure they weren't really looking at you like that."

"Oh yeah. They were. Whatever. I guess it'll pass. Eventually. Then when I got hold of my mom, I discovered she's on Greenbush Island."

"You're kidding."

"Nope. Apparently she was just getting off the ferry when we were getting on. Okay, maybe not, but we must have just missed each other. And what's even more weird? She's with Owen Ralston."

"Allie's dad?"

He laughed at her saying the same thing he had. "Yup."

"Whoa. What are they doing together?"

"I decided I don't want to know."

"They've been friends a long time."

"No. Mom and Lily were friends."

"You know what I mean."

He sighed. "Yeah. I guess I just don't want to think of my mom...uh..."

"Hey." She reached over and squeezed his hand. "I know how you feel. Seeing my dad with Susan was a little freaky. But I guess...they have a right to move on, and have relationships with other people."

He nodded. "I guess you're right. Speaking of your dad, what was up with him?"

"I went down to the marina to see him, and he was fighting with an Excel spreadsheet. Apparently Hal retired a few months ago. I didn't even know. So Dad's been trying to do the books himself. I said I'd help him while I'm here."

"Hey. I thought you were going to help me?"

She looked at him. He met her eyes. He couldn't stop the smile that tugged his lips, and he watched her mouth curve in response. "I'm just so in demand," she murmured. "Unfortunately not by Engblun and Seabrook."

He shook his head. "Their loss, Dev. Seriously." And then he leaned over and kissed her.

She tasted of blackberries and spice and wine, rich and warm. Like temptation and longing, comfort and excitement. His mouth moved on hers and she kissed him back, her lips clinging to his in a long, heated kiss. Lust shot through him and his groin tightened.

He drew back slowly. He dipped his index finger into his

glass of wine and painted it over her full bottom lip. Then he leaned forward and licked it off. She moaned.

"I don't know much about wine," he murmured. "But I think this is the best I've ever had."

He sucked briefly on her lip and then moved away again.

"I think I have to agree," she said, her voice husky.

"Know what would make it even better?"

"What?"

"Licking it off your body."

Her eyes darkened and her eyelids went heavy. "Mmm."

"And then drinking the rest of it while we have a bath in my tub."

Her lips parted, and he caught the hungry gleam in her eyes. "That sounds...zinful."

"Cute. Take off your clothes."

Chapter Fifteen

He took her glass of wine from her and set it on the bedside table, holding her gaze the entire time. She rose and slowly pulled her T-shirt over her head, then undid her jeans. She shifted her hips from side to side as she pushed them down, and Josh's eyes darkened. She smiled.

"You too," she said softly, and he reached behind his neck and yanked his own T-shirt off. Soon they were both naked and stretched out on the bed, legs entwined, bodies pressed together. He kissed her jaw, opened his mouth on the side of her neck and gently sucked, then shifted his body lower to lick a trail of heat over her throat. He kissed her chest, then her breasts. Excitement once again pooled low down inside her, warmth spreading through her body. He cupped one breast and lifted it to his mouth, and when his lips closed over the tender tip, a shudder of pleasure shook her to her core. He suckled at it with firm pressure, sending currents of sensation between her thighs. Her hands came up to his head, holding him there at her breast as he moved from one nipple to the other, grazing her with his teeth, then closing his lips over her tightened flesh. Her breasts felt swollen and heavy, her pelvis achy with need.

"You have such beautiful breasts," he murmured, kissing the inner curve of one. "Such pretty nipples." His tongue licked over one of them, and she shivered at both his words and his touch.

He rolled away from her, and she watched in a daze as he reached for the glass of red wine. Then he dipped his fingers into the wine and rubbed them over one nipple. The cool wetness made her flesh pucker up even more. He bent his head to lick over her breast, his eyes heavy-lidded as he tasted her and the wine.

"Mmm," he murmured. "I was right."

He let drops of wine fall from his fingertips onto the other breast and licked and sucked it too, until she was writhing with need. Then he kissed between her breasts and shifted his body lower still, kissing her tummy, her navel, and then the patch of hair at the apex of her thighs.

Her body tightened in anticipation, every nerve ending electrified, and a whimper slipped past her lips.

"Wanna taste you, baby," he said against the skin of her hip. He still held the wineglass and lifted it. Was he going to actually pour it on her? Because that was going to make a really big mess. But no...

"I'll save that for when we're in the tub," he murmured, setting the glass back on the table.

He licked the crease at her groin, and then his big hands landed on her inner thighs and gently parted them. She looked down her body at his head and wide shoulders between her legs, and her stomach did another lusty flip.

He took his time, drawing out the expectation, building the hunger inside her as she struggled to draw air into her lungs. He studied her with an absorbed expression on his face, just visible in the shadowy bedroom, and her insides twisted while heat built in her womb. Then he lowered his head and pressed a kiss to her folds, a soft, closed-mouth kiss, then another and another down the seam.

"So soft." His voice came to her ears through a fog of delight. He brushed his fingertips over her. "Love that you're still bare here. Your skin is just so soft."

He'd been the one who convinced her to wax there, and now she was glad she'd kept with it.

His thumbs parted her then, and his kisses grew deeper, his mouth opening on her and sucking gently, one side, then the other, his tongue brushing over her sensitive flesh. He licked up. Then down. Slowly. Tasting her. Her clit ached, but he didn't touch it, just licked around it, then tongued his way back down. He dipped into her opening, rubbed his tongue over swollen tissues there, nibbled at her thighs, kissed his way back up.

"God, Dev. I love how wet you get." He lapped again at her with agonizing gentleness, her entire body buzzing now with the need for a firmer touch. More soft sounds escaped her, little, begging sounds. "And you taste so sweet." He licked more.

She lifted her hips in needy supplication, and he slipped his hands beneath her butt and held her there. Her legs fell open wide as he lifted her to his mouth. She closed her eyes and her head sank into the pillow as she lost herself in the feel of his tongue sliding over her flesh, his fingers digging into her ass, his whiskers abrading her thighs. Sensation whipped through her body. "Please," she managed to cry. "Please, Josh."

She felt his smile against her, his tongue pushing deep inside her again, so good, but not quite enough, not deep enough, not hard enough, and her clit pulsed with maddening exigency. She dug her fingers into his hair, her nails scraping on his scalp, and his groan rumbled against her.

One of his thumbs slipped into her cream, then rubbed down from her vagina, and she jerked against his hands and his mouth, and again cried out.

"Sssh," he murmured. "Sssh. You like this."

God, she did, so much. Nobody else had ever touched her there, before Josh or after him, and her entire body seized with excitement. Her head rolled on the pillow, and her hands moved to her breasts.

"Oh god yeah," he groaned. "That's so hot. Touch yourself,

baby."

She plucked at her nipples as he ate her with lips and tongue and teeth and then finally, dear god, *finally*, he licked over her straining clit. She gasped. As he tongued the sensitive nub back and forth, his thumb teased, and pleasure intensified, multiplied. A small wail fell from her lips. Heat coiled inside her, hot and tight, twisting and building, hotter and higher, her entire body consumed with it. His thumb inside her moved, sending sparkles of sensation surging through her body. She squeezed her breasts, Josh's tongue on her clit creating buzzing heat in her veins, spreading from her center to her fingertips and toes and scalp.

"Don't stop," she gasped. "Please don't stop...just...like...that..." And with another low wail, the pleasure reached its peak and she went over, her hips lifting, her heels digging into the mattress. Wave after wave of sensation washed over her, and she couldn't stop the noises she made as she came against his mouth. He kept up the pressure on her clit, prolonging the orgasm almost painfully, until her body lay limp and exhausted.

He kissed her thighs, her hips, her tummy again, making soft, appreciative noises as he moved back up her body and then finally kissed her mouth. She tasted herself as her tongue slid over his, and she moaned. His hand pushed into her hair, and he pressed his cheek against hers.

"Jesus," he muttered. "You're amazing."

"I'm amazing?" She could barely form words, could barely lift her eyelids. "You're the one who just took me apart. Jeebus Crust."

"Okay. That made me so fucking hard. Need a condom."

"Did you get some?"

"Oh yeah." He reached for the small drawer of the night table. She lay there catching her breath while he rolled one on.

"I don't know if I can move," she said.

He grinned and slid over her. "That's okay. I'll do the moving this time."

She gave him a slow smile back as he knelt between her legs, lifting her knees. She looked down at him, the condom stretched thin and tight over his girth. He stroked the head of his cock through her slick folds, still so sensitive. She groaned.

"Oh yeah," he said. "See what I mean? You're so damn wet. That makes me nuts, Dev."

"Good."

They shared a heated, special smile, and then he pushed into her. Her body stretched to accommodate him, a brief, burning pain searing her as he entered her. Her passage clenched around him. With his knees spread wide, he gently slid in deeper, and deeper. She tried to breathe, watched where their bodies were joined, breathless at the beauty of his body, the V of his torso so wide at the shoulders and chest, tapering down to narrow waist and hips, his abs rippling, his biceps flexing as he held her legs. The thick column of flesh slid in and out of her, the dark hair at his groin male and erotic as it pressed against her.

He filled her so deliciously, stroking over electrified nerve endings, so deep, so full. The pressure of him inside her bordered on pain, but the sweetest pain. He released her legs and reached for her waist, holding her body as his thrusts grew harder and faster. His eyes darkened, watching her so intently. The eye contact they shared increased the intimacy to an almost unbearable level of pleasure and connection.

She lifted into him, meeting his strokes, finding the energy despite her words about being unable to move. It wasn't as if she even had to try—her body just responded to him instinctively, seeking the friction they both needed. His gaze fell to her breasts, and then he moved over her to take one nipple into his mouth. He drew on it with long, hard pulls, making her tighten up around him in ecstasy, and he groaned, a low growl of such pleasure it sent another thrill through her.

She reached for his shoulders and hung on for dear life, sensation whipping around inside her all hot and wild. He sucked on her nipples, kissed her breasts, then fell over her and buried his face in the side of her neck. With some of his weight on his elbows, his body still pressed her into the mattress with erotic weight, his hips flexing to move his shaft in and out, and she wrapped her legs around him as well as her arms, holding him close, as close as they could possibly be. One of his hands slid beneath her head, coming around to her forehead to push her hair off her face, and he lifted his head to look down at her, his eyes blazing. They moved together, urgent, straining, staring into each other's eyes.

I love you, I love you, I love you.

The words shocked her even though she was nearly mindless with pleasure. Had she said them out loud? Oh god. She bit her lip, and her fingers dug into his resilient flesh, his taut muscles, as he pressed into her again and again, taking her up higher...and then she went over. She cried out helplessly as her body shuddered with the violence of her orgasm, intense, pure rapture exploding inside her and ripping through her body.

Since Josh had a twenty-four-hour shift from Sunday morning till Monday morning, Devon spent most of the day Sunday at the marina, having a look at the books for her dad's business. Things were in pretty good shape since it had only been a few months since Hal retired, but she could see that her dad was falling behind with it. And she could also see that he was relieved that she was doing this, even though he didn't really say much.

The charter business was busy as they moved into the height of the tourist season. Devon stayed mostly in the office at the back while the two teenagers Dad had hired for the summer dealt with customers up front, and Dad and his other staff took the boats out. A couple of times when things got busy, she'd stepped in to help. Strangely, she knew exactly what to do, as if it had been yesterday she'd last worked there, all the knowledge from those summers she'd worked still there in her head. Focusing on all that took her mind off Josh and the evening they'd spent together at his place. The sinful...er, zinful...things they'd done with that wine and the decadent bath they'd taken together after.

It also took her thoughts off the reminder she'd had the evening before that Josh and Allie had been about to move in together. They'd been about to get married. That was the house Josh and Allie were going to live together in. She'd had more than one moment of wondering what she was doing there and what was happening between her and Josh. And more than one moment of wondering if she shouldn't just leave Promise Harbor and go back to Boston.

She wasn't sure why she didn't, except the thought of going back to her empty apartment and spending lonely days searching for a job depressed the hell out of her. Along with the thought of not seeing Josh again. She had a feeling she'd gotten herself in a little trouble here.

That evening after they'd eaten dinner, Susan dropped over with dessert, an apple pie she'd made.

"Thanks," Devon said coolly, still not sure how she felt about this whole relationship between Susan and her father.

Susan set the pie on the counter and reached for a knife to cut it. Huh. Pretty much at home there.

"There's some vanilla ice cream in the freezer," Susan said cheerfully. "I'm going to have some with my pie. Anyone else?"

Devon narrowed her eyes. How'd she know there was vanilla ice cream in the freezer?

"I'll have ice cream," Dad said, heading to the freezer.

Devon sat there watching them move around the kitchen together, exchanging smiles again.

Susan cut the pie and slid the pieces onto plates while Dad scooped out ice cream. "How long are you going to be here, Devon?" she asked.

"I don't know, actually." She slid her bottom lip between her teeth. "I...lost my job."

"Oh no!" Susan turned to look at her. "When did that happen?"

"Weeks ago." She met Susan's eyes and knew what she was thinking. But the soft warmth on Susan's face didn't condemn her for keeping that information to herself. Instead, she saw understanding. "I've been looking for something else, but there's not a lot out there."

"Looking for a new job is hard," Susan said. And that simple statement made Devon feel...okay.

Susan set a plate in front of her, then set another one for herself and sat, and Dad joined them.

"Sometimes it's good to have a break," Susan said.

"I suppose." Devon relaxed a little at Susan's easy acceptance of her being there without much of an explanation. "This pie is really good. Thanks for bringing it over."

"My pleasure."

When they'd finished their pie, Dad said, "I'm going for a walk." He looked at Susan. Not at her. Devon bent her head.

"Would you like to join us, Devon?" Susan asked.

Devon's head snapped up and she met Susan's eyes. The soft smile and understanding made her insides quiver. She hesitated, but shook her head. "No thanks. You go on."

Josh arrived at the firehouse well before the start of the eight o'clock shift to check in with the off-going shift before they left, and at eight sharp he had his own shift lined up in the apparatus room for roll call and to give everyone their assignments for the day—which engine they were on, who was driving, all that stuff—and to go over the day's schedule. A schedule which of course could change in a heartbeat depending on what calls came in.

He then headed to his office to log personnel and equipment, verify training and inspection schedules and take care of all the other endless administrative duties, while the rest of the team began to check out each fire engine and piece of equipment to make sure they were fully operational, and also do some cleaning. Around ten o'clock he pushed away from the computer. Time for a workout.

Fitness was important and necessary in his job, and he worked hard to maintain the strength he needed to be able to haul someone out of a burning building, to carry the weight of oxygen tanks on his back, to chop through the roof of a burning house to create a hole large enough to allow heat, smoke and gases to escape so the ground crew could do their work. As he pumped some iron, he joked around with the other guys, who at first were cautious and unsure of what to say to him after what had happened at the wedding. But they loosened up a little and things edged back to normal, with easy insults flying back and forth.

Some of the guys, his buddies, had been at the wedding. Some hadn't. But damn, they were a good bunch of guys to work with. He wiped some sweat off his forehead, smiling.

"So what did you do on your honeymoon, Captain?" Matt asked. "I mean, your holiday."

Josh grinned. "I did go on the honeymoon. I'd booked a suite at the Oceanside Inn on Greenbush Island, so I went anyway."

"No shit. All by yourself?"

Was that innocent, or was he fishing? Josh eyed him. "Ah...not exactly." Okay, what the hell was he supposed to say about that? "A friend came with me."

"Huh. Jackson?"

"No. An old friend who'd been at the wedding."

Antonio smiled slyly at him. "I heard a rumor you were buying an expensive bottle of wine for a lady last night. Didn't take you long to get over being jilted."

"Christ, it doesn't take long for rumors to start in this town." Josh shook his head.

But Antonio had noticed he hadn't really responded. "Nice deflection," he said, dropping the weights he held.

Josh grinned but said nothing. Out of respect for both Devon and Allie, it didn't seem right to be telling the guys what had happened. He wasn't sure yet where things were going with Devon, but the longer she stayed around, the more chance there was that people were going to find out. Jackson knew who he'd been with, but he trusted Jackson to keep his mouth shut.

Then he was saved by the bell, literally, as a call came in.

The rest of the day was divided between responding to calls involving a cardiac arrest, a kitchen fire and a vehicle fire, and the rest of the maintenance and training that had to be done. And thinking about Devon.

Thinking about how tough she tried to be. He'd known about what had happened with her mother, of course, but he hadn't realized just how affected she'd been by that. And though he'd known she and her dad weren't close, he'd had no idea that she thought her father hated her. Why had she never told him that stuff before?

He knew the answer. He knew how much she hated being

pitied. Christ. He shook his head. She'd always been spunky and determined, never letting things get her down, and he'd always loved that about her. She'd always had a sense of humor, even when things weren't going well. Looking back, he could see how many times she'd just picked up and carried on when things went wrong, and he'd admired that, but now he had to wonder how many times she'd kept her real feelings all locked up inside her. All those times she'd told him she was fine—maybe she hadn't been.

Like the conversation she'd had with Allie. She'd said she'd been fine with him and Allie dating. But deep inside, had she been hurt? By both of them? Christ, it was a double betrayal, and he ached with regret for that. And what about when she'd told him he should go back to Promise Harbor to be with his family and look after them and she'd be fine?

Josh slammed a hand down on his desk, startling one of the paramedics in the office.

"Uh...everything okay, Captain?" Antonio asked.

Josh grimaced and rubbed his face. Adrenaline surged through him, and his body tingled with the need to jump up and do something. Dammit, he needed to go fight a fire or something. "Yeah," he said. "Sorry."

Chapter Sixteen

Josh picked Devon up at her dad's place, and they drove out to Brewster Landscaping on Monday afternoon. She'd always enjoyed going to the greenhouses there in the spring to buy bedding plants. When Josh had worked summers planting trees and shrubs and mowing grass, she'd been selling fishing tackle, and even though she loved the ocean, she'd often thought how nice it would be to work where you were surrounded by the beauty and color and fragrance of plants and flowers instead of...fish.

Things were busy in the greenhouse, lots of people using the beautiful June day to buy flowers and pots and gardening tools. She inhaled the fresh green and floral scents as they walked past rows of hanging baskets overflowing with petunias, verbena, lobelia and ivy, past shelves stocked with ridiculous garden gnomes, and into the offices at the back of the building.

Everyone greeted Josh with smiles, but she could see the carefulness in their eyes. "Hey, welcome back," a woman said.

Devon watched two other women exchange glances.

"Thanks," Josh said, looking around. Then he sighed. "Okay, let's get it over with. Yes, Allie walked out on the wedding."

"I heard she was carried out," a man said. The others made small sounds of disapproval at his forthrightness.

Josh just laughed. "Yeah. Actually, that's true. She was carried. But before you start talking about her being kidnapped, I can assure you she left of her own free will. And yes, before you ask, I'm fine." He held up his hands. "Seriously." He turned to Devon. "Everyone, this is Devon Grant. She's an investment banker and knows some things about money. She's got some ideas about how to improve our cash flow." He introduced the staff to her, a blur of names and faces she wouldn't remember right away. "Come on in here." He led the way into a small office. "Devon, this is Bill, our manager. Bill, Devon Grant." He repeated the explanation of why she was there. Bill nodded, seeming a little taken aback. Maybe he thought she was after his job.

"So how do we get started on this financing thing?" Josh asked. "I feel totally lost when it comes to things like that."

"That's okay. That's what I'm here for. After I have a look at your accounts receivable, I'll contact a factoring company. I know a few good ones. Then they'll have a look at your credit and your clients' credit history. They'll notify your customers to pay them, and they'll take responsibility for collection of payments. This puts the risk of nonpayment fully on them."

Josh frowned. "They're going to contact our customers?"

"Yes."

"I don't know if I like that. Will they think we're having financial problems?"

"No, I don't think so. Lots of businesses have cash flow that varies, like yours. When you have a busy summer season, the money is coming in, but you need to cover short-term cash needs in slower periods, like the winter. It's not that unusual."

"That's true," Bill said. "We've been focusing on trying to collect faster, trying to offer early payment incentives."

"Two percent discount?" Devon said.

"Yeah. But we're pretty much at the mercy of our customers when it comes to cash flow."

Devon gave a wry smile and nodded. "I hear you."

"I'll let you two talk money," Josh said. "I'm going to go see what else needs to be done."

She was happy to focus on business matters, things that she was familiar with and knowledgeable about, things she loved, and she and Bill got to work. Time flew by until Josh came back into the office. She glanced at her watch and saw it was after five o'clock.

"How's it going?" he asked, leaning on the desk. He'd been out in the sun, his hair tousled by the wind, his face tanned, his clothes dusty and his hands dirty. He looked hot. And not just temperature.

"Good."

"Where's Bill? Gone home?"

"No. He just went to the photocopier, I think."

"Ready to call it a day?"

"I guess I am." She stretched her arms over her head, and when she noticed Josh's eyes drop to her breasts, heat washed over her.

"You need to fill out some forms so we can pay you."

She paused. "You don't have to pay me for this."

He frowned. "Of course I do."

"I'm just helping you out."

"Devon, for Chrissake. I'm paying you for your time. You're like a...consultant. They charge big bucks."

"The reason I'm here is your cash flow problem," she said pointedly, raising an eyebrow.

He grinned. "Oh yeah."

She couldn't resist the smile that tugged at her lips.

"I'm still paying you," he said. "It's not that we're not making money, Dev. It's cash flow."

"Okay," she conceded. "But you don't need to feel sorry for

me. I know I said I'm broke, but I...okay, I'm broke, but still..."

He laughed. "Give it up. Take the money."

She huffed. "Fine."

"Etta does the payroll stuff. We'll talk to her tomorrow. Now, come to my place for dinner."

Josh had two days off, so he didn't have to get up early, and they lingered in bed in the morning. Then he got up and went downstairs to make coffee before disappearing into the bathroom for a shower. Devon smiled and stretched in his big bed, burying her face in Josh's pillow and inhaling his scent, then climbed out of bed. They planned to go back to Brewster Landscaping today to do more work on getting the financing set up.

She ventured downstairs, following the delicious scent of the coffee, and poured herself a cup. Carrying the mug, she wandered around the house, morning sun filling the big rooms with light. It was such a great house. She could picture wooden blinds on the windows, rugs on the hardwood floors and the kind of furniture she'd like to fill the empty rooms with. She stopped and frowned at some boxes and a big plastic garbage bag sitting on the floor in what would be the dining room, if he had a dining table. Garbage? That wasn't good. She opened the loosely tied bag and peered in. No. Not garbage. She tugged out a small hooded sweatshirt, obviously a woman's. A bottle of conditioner. A little pink shaver.

Her heart plummeted to her toes as she realized what she was looking at. Allie's things.

Oh fishsticks.

Of course Allie had probably spent a lot of time at Josh's place. They'd been getting married. She sucked on a suddenly trembling bottom lip as she pushed the things back into the bag

198

and retied it. Then she sank to the floor and sat there for a moment, staring blindly across the room.

Why did this bother her so much? It certainly was no surprise. Maybe she'd managed to forget, even just a little, that Josh had been about to marry another woman not that long ago, but this was a very real and tangible reminder. Allie. And that hurt returned and spread outward from the sharp ache in her stomach.

She bowed her head and glumly regarded the floor. What was going on with her and Josh now? She'd been feeling all...good. Helping him. Feeling needed and...and...cared for. But how could that be?

God, she'd been crazy to agree to come back to the harbor and spend more time with him. She was only going to get hurt again.

The crazy thing was, at that moment she so wished she had someone to talk to about this. Someone she trusted with all her being, someone she trusted so much she could tell that person anything. Someone like a best friend. Someone like Allie.

But she and Allie weren't best friends anymore.

She pushed to her feet and gulped some of the hot coffee, the heat easing the ache in her throat. This tangible reminder of how close Josh and Allie had been to getting married and making their relationship permanent wasn't something she'd wanted to come across, but maybe it was a good thing. She needed reminders of why she should not be getting involved with Josh again. She shouldn't have spent the night with him.

She wanted to run. Heat raced through her veins and her heart sped up. But she couldn't leave—she had no car. She drew in a long breath. She also couldn't run because she'd told Josh she would help him with the business, and now she had to follow through on that.

She heard the water stop running upstairs, and

straightening her shoulders, she climbed the steps back up to the bedroom. She walked in just as Josh emerged from the bathroom naked, water droplets clinging to his tanned shoulders, running over big rounded muscles. He rubbed a towel over his hair. Her insides squeezed hard.

He didn't even hesitate to walk toward her, and she blinked when he took the cup of coffee from her hands. "Thanks," he said, flashing a twinkling look at her as he lifted it to his mouth.

Her heart softened. "Hey!" she said, scowling. "That's mine!"

"And here I thought you were looking after me and bringing me coffee." He grinned.

She tried to harden her heart again, but holy cheese and crackers, it was hard in the face of his naked beauty and easy teasing.

"Get dressed," she said, turning away. "We need to get to work."

"Me get dressed?" he said. "How about you? You're not exactly dressed for the office."

She'd slipped on one of his T-shirts. "True," she said. "Damn. I'm going to have to wear the same clothes." She'd just worn jeans and a tank top yesterday, but today if she wore her sweater over it, maybe it wouldn't be so noticeable.

"Do you want to go home first?" he asked. "We can swing by there on the way."

She paused with her hands on the hem of the T-shirt. "Really?"

"Of course." He sauntered up to her, and the sexy scent of his shower gel enveloped her. "Whatever you want, Dev." He bent his head and kissed her. She closed her eyes against the overwhelming wave of affection and gratitude that swept over her. She broke away from the kiss.

He stepped back, eyeing her, and she once again gave him her back as she dressed.

Her dad had already left for the marina. Josh waited in the small kitchen while she hurried into the bedroom to change. She didn't have a lot of wardrobe to choose from, and certainly not anything she'd ever worn to the office in Boston, but the landscaping company was a totally different environment. When she emerged dressed in her striped cotton skirt and pink tank top, he gave her a sexy up-and-down look of appreciation.

Her heart missed a beat, but she ignored the look.

"Very pretty," he said, moving closer.

She sidestepped him. "I need more coffee. Can we stop somewhere and pick one up?"

After a short pause, he said, "Sure. We'll stop at Starbucks."

"There's a Starbucks in the harbor?"

"Yeah, apparently for a couple of years now."

She cast him a quick glance and caught the puzzlement in his eyes before they left the house.

With grande coffees in hand, they made most of the drive out to Brewster Landscaping in silence.

"What are you up to today?" she asked, looking out the side window at the shrub-lined estuary they were passing.

"I'm not sure. I'll see what needs to be done, but if things are under control I might head home and start scraping paint off the outside of the house."

"Sounds like fun."

"Someone's gotta do it. I should also give Jackson a call and see what's up with him."

He was such a hard worker. Another thing she'd loved about him.

Devon was deep into spreadsheets and numbers when a voice spoke from the open door of the office.

"How's it going?"

She looked up to see Karla, to whom Josh had introduced her yesterday. "Good, thanks," she said with a smile, leaning back in her chair.

"Would you like to join us for lunch? Liz and I are going over to Sloppy Joe's."

Surprise kept her from answering immediately, but then warmth washed over her. "That would be nice," she said slowly. "I didn't even realize it was lunch time."

"It's almost one," Karla said, "But Liz and I like to take a late lunch."

Devon grabbed her purse and rose from the chair. She followed the other two women out to the parking lot, and they climbed into Liz's Dodge Caravan for the short drive. At the restaurant, they elected to sit outside on the small patio where picnic tables had been arranged.

"Lucky for the breeze today," Liz commented, unwrapping her sandwich. "So it's not too hot here."

Mounds of white clouds floated in the blue sky, occasionally blocking out the sun. Devon slid her sunglasses on as the sun emerged, and picked up her own sandwich.

Karla and Liz talked about Karla's son's baseball game the evening before and how Liz was annoyed at her husband because he'd just spent seven hundred dollars on a rare Pez dispenser to add to his collection, and Devon relaxed until they turned their attention to her.

"You're from the harbor, aren't you?" Liz asked.

"Yes. I left to go to college, about ten years ago."

She estimated Liz and Karla were in their thirties, enough years older than her that she wouldn't know them from school, but not old enough to be her father's age.

"Where do you live now?"

"Boston."

"Just here on vacation?" She read the curiosity in Karla's eyes.

"Sort of. I came back for Josh and Allie's wedding."

"Oooooh. We heard about that. Poor Josh."

"What kind of woman would ditch *Josh* at the altar?" Liz said, shaking her head.

"I think it's kind of romantic," Karla said. "Being carried out like that by the love of her life."

Love of her life? Gavin? Huh. Devon wasn't so sure about that, but whatever.

"Romantic for her." Liz snorted. "Not so much for Josh. He's such a great guy. He doesn't deserve that."

"How do you know Josh?" Karla asked conversationally.

Devon looked down at her food. "Allie Ralston and I were best friends growing up. I met Josh through her. Their families are close."

"Oh yes, they are." The women exchanged glances.

Devon shifted on the wooden bench of the picnic table and searched for some other topic. "How old are your kids?" she asked the two women. That worked well since they apparently loved talking about their kids, and the remainder of the lunch was spent discussing them and various community activities both women and their families were involved in. Devon found herself interested in knowing what was happening in Promise Harbor, laughing at their sense of humor and the comments they made about some of the people who lived there.

"I can't believe I didn't know Marbell Jacobs isn't the mayor anymore," she said with a laugh.

"She turned ninety in April," Karla said. "I guess it was

getting a bit much for her."

"I think she could still do it," Liz said. "She's still sharp as a clam shell."

"Connie Stone is a very popular mayor, though," Karla said.

When they were back at the office, Devon said, "Thanks for inviting me along. That was fun."

And she meant it.

Bill brought her some forms to fill out so they could pay her, including one for her to track her hours. "Josh told me you might not want to sign these," he said. "But he said to make sure you did."

Devon wasn't going to give Bill a hard time about it, so she just took the forms with a smile and set them aside to fill out later. Then she dived back into the books of the business.

This was such a different environment to work in than Englun and Seabrook on the twenty-fifth floor of the Liberty Building in downtown Boston, with its fierce competition, high-stakes deals and intense pressure. She and Bill got talking about the books. Bill was a nice guy, but she could see there were some gaps in how things were being handled.

Josh showed up at four o'clock, apparently having showered and changed, his hair damp, dressed in jeans and a navy T-shirt that hugged his broad chest. "You had enough here yet?" he asked her as he leaned on the desk.

She stretched back in her chair. "I suppose. My boss is a tyrant, though."

He grinned. "Bill's being a tyrant?" He glanced at the other desk, where Bill sat. Bill laughed.

"I meant you. I guess I'm done for today."

"She's smart," Bill told him. "Really smart. She helped me with a bunch of stuff today."

Josh studied her and heat washed over her. She lifted one

shoulder and dropped her eyes.

"I know she's smart," he said. "Thanks, Dev."

Bill rose from his desk and, with a salute, left them alone in the small office.

"I contacted a couple of factoring companies and got things started," Dev said.

"Great." Josh blew out a breath and tipped his head back. "You have no idea what a relief it is to have some of this taken off my shoulders. Seriously—thank you."

"But you have such nice broad shoulders," she murmured, eyeing them appreciatively as she stood. "Those are superhero shoulders."

A smile tugged his lips, but he shook his head. "I told you, I'm no superhero. Come on. I want to take you out for dinner."

She froze. "Out for dinner?"

"Yeah. Where would you like to go? Barney's Chowder House? Or somewhere nicer? Maybe the Waterfront?"

"We can't go out for dinner."

His eyebrows pulled together above his nose. "Why not?"

"Someone might see us."

His forehead furrowed even more. "So?"

"You know how people talk in this town."

"Again...so?"

Her stomach tightened. "Josh, look. I'm leaving soon. Let's not get things all stirred up for nothing. You'll be staying, and you're the one that will have to deal with it all."

He stared at her.

"What?" She touched her hair.

"You're leaving soon."

Chapter Seventeen

"Well...yes." Devon swallowed. "You knew that. I said I'd come back for a while and help you get things sorted out with the cash flow and get the factoring set up, but I told you, I...I can't stay here." Her throat constricted a little. She watched him watching her, his eyes serious and intent.

"Why not, Dev?"

She blinked. And blinked again. Her skin went cold. Her palms grew clammy. "Because I live in Boston."

He tipped his head to one side. "These last few days..." He paused. His throat worked as he swallowed. "I don't want you to leave, Devon."

Her stomach cramped up even more. It was like déjà vu, except this time she was the one leaving. And wasn't that better?

Not really. It sucked.

She pressed her lips together to stop them from trembling. "I have to leave. I have to go back to Boston and find a job."

"I'll give you a job here," he said slowly. He moved closer, and she resisted the urge to step back. Not because she didn't want him to touch her or get closer...but because she did, so, so much. "These last few days...last week on the island...it's been amazing being with you again, Dev." He reached out to stroke her hair back from her face, and her body tensed. "Hasn't it? For you too?"

Her throat so tight she could barely breathe, she nodded and tried for a light smile. "Of course. It was fun."

"It was more than fun." A crease appeared again between his eyebrows. "You know it was. Dev...what we had together. I still care about you."

"You were going to marry someone else," she whispered.

He glanced around. Bill hadn't come back and they were still alone, but... "Do we have to have this conversation here?"

Probably not the best place to do this. She gave a tight shake of her head.

"Come on." He held her arm lightly and led the way out of the office, back through the greenhouse and out the front doors into the parking lot. His Honda CR-V was parked on the far side and they walked across the lot, gravel crunching beneath their feet. Dev tried to relax her throat and her constricted lungs and breathe. Her heart tapped out an uneven rhythm in her chest.

He shouldn't be saying things like that. He shouldn't be. She shouldn't have gotten involved with him again. She shouldn't have gone with him to the island, despite her desperate desire to find William Mudge.

When they were seated in his vehicle, he turned his head and looked at her. "Where to?"

She had no idea. She didn't want to go back to his place, because even the few hours she'd spent there had her getting all attached to it, imagining things that she couldn't have. She didn't want to go to a restaurant and make a scene, or start people talking about them. That left... "Let's go to my dad's place," she said with a sigh.

"Will he be home?"

"Not yet."

Josh nodded, reversed the truck and exited the parking lot with a small burst of gravel beneath his tires as he trod on the gas. She fidgeted with the strap of her purse. He wasn't happy and she didn't blame him. Her insides twisted into knots.

She watched his fingers grip the wheel, glanced surreptitiously at his tense chin and the grim line of his mouth. She opened her mouth to say something, then shut it again and looked down at her hands clasped around her purse strap. Damn.

Josh parked on the street in front of Dad's place, and she let them in with the key she now kept on her key ring. The small house smelled faintly of Susan's cranberry-scented candle, and the silence retreated as they walked into the kitchen, Josh's footsteps heavy, hers lighter on the vinyl flooring. She sent him a quick glance. "Would you like something to drink? I'm sure Dad has beer, or something..."

He shook his head. "No. Thanks."

She lifted her chin and led them into the living room. She turned to face him. "Josh, please don't do this."

She caught the glint of anger in his eyes, the way his jaw tensed. "Do what?"

"I don't want to do this again," she whispered to his chest. *It hurt so much the last time.*

"You're the one who's leaving," he pointed out, moving closer. The scent of his shower gel and shampoo teased her senses, and the warmth of his body heated her chilled skin. "But then, you're really the one who left last time, aren't you?"

Her head snapped up and she stared at him. "What?"

His eyes narrowed a little as he looked down at her. "I said you're really the one who left."

"That doesn't make any sense," she protested, her voice husky. "*You're* the one who left. You're the one who had to move back to Promise Harbor to look after your family. And..." She swallowed. "Allie. And her family."

"I wanted you to come with me."

Her lips trembled. "But I couldn't."

He closed his eyes briefly. "Okay. You're right. We don't have to go through that all again. What happened, happened. But this is now, Devon. Things are different now."

"What's different?" Her voice started to climb. "Nothing's different. You still have your family to look after. I still have my life in Boston."

"You don't have a job anymore," he pointed out. "That was your main reason for staying there. Wasn't it?"

"Um. Yes. But..."

"I said I'd give you a job."

She frowned at him. Yes, he had said that, but good god, he didn't need to take pity on her to that extent. "I'll find a job," she said with grim determination. "When I get back to Boston. It's been tough, but I'll be okay, Josh." She knew she was a somewhat pathetic figure, having lost her job and not being able to find one, and then that humiliating episode with William Mudge... She never should have broken down and cried in front of Josh. Now he was offering her a job, for heaven's sake!

"Oh for... I have no doubt you could find a job if you went back there. I'm trying to tell you, I want you to stay here. Let me help you, Dev."

Help her. "That's not what I want," she whispered. "That's not the kind of job I want."

He made a sound low in his throat. "Yeah. I know. Once again, not good enough for you. Right?"

"No! That's not it!" She stared at him open-mouthed. "Josh..."

He reached for her, his hands sliding onto her hips to pull her closer, and once more she felt that urge to just throw herself into his arms, to just let go, let it all go, let it all out...but she couldn't.

She stiffened and turned her face away from him.

"Devon." His voice went low and smoky. He pressed his face to her hair. "Please, Devon. I love you."

Oh. Jeebus. Cripes.

Her heart exploded into a rapid rhythm that stole her breath. A small sound escaped her, and she pressed her lips together and closed her eyes. *I love you too.*

"I don't want to lose you again," he murmured against her hair. "We can make things work here."

How could he say things like that? Did he not know how dangerous it was? He was crazy to trust her with things like that, because he should know she was only going to hurt him.

"It won't work," she said, pulling away from him. Her heart felt like a dozen knives were stabbing into it over and over. She rubbed her hands up and down her arms as she stepped back. "It won't work. I was crazy to come back here. I don't need you to help me, Josh."

His face tightened into lines so stark and agonized the pain in her heart got even worse. Her breath panted in and out in short little puffs, not getting enough oxygen to her, and her head went light. She felt frozen. Stiff. Paralyzed.

"I guess I'll go then," he said, his voice almost unrecognizable. "Let me know how that works out for you, Dev." He turned just as the sound of the back door opening reached them.

Susan's light laugh carried into the living room. "Oh Doug. It's fine, I'm sure."

Dad appeared in the arched doorway. "Oh hey," he said. "I saw your vehicle out front, Josh."

Susan appeared behind him with a saucy smile. "He was afraid of what he might be interrupting."

Then her smile faded as she took in Josh's expression and both she and Dad sensed the chowder-thick tension in the room.

"I was just leaving," Josh said woodenly. "Nice to see you." He headed to the front door and pushed out through it, shutting it behind him with a bang.

Devon stared after him, her heart still thudding painfully, then turned her gaze to Dad and Susan. An awkward silence filled the space around them.

"Did you two fight about something?" Susan asked carefully.

"You could say that." Her lips felt stiff and cold. She shook her head. "I...I..." She fought the sob that crawled up her throat. "I'm going back to Boston."

Susan and Dad exchanged a glance. "Now?"

She hadn't really thought that all out. She glanced at her watch. "Sure. Yeah. Why not?" Early evening left plenty of time for the drive back to the city. "Just have to p-pack my things."

"I thought you were helping Josh at Brewster Landscaping?" Dad said. "I thought you were going to help *me*."

She shook her head. "I can't. I have to go." She edged toward the door, but they were blocking her from dashing down the hall to her bedroom.

Dad frowned. "Devon. Never mind me. I'll manage. But if you told Josh you were going to do something for him, you damn well better do it."

She gaped at him. "Dad! I can't stay. I can't!"

"Oh, Devon," Susan said, her voice soft. "Come here." She held out her arms. Oh fishsticks, it was so tempting to move into the offer of a hug. Because sometimes a hug just felt so good. But Susan wasn't her mother, in fact she hardly knew her, and Devon just shook her head. Susan's face fell.

"Please," Devon said. "I have to go."

"You still love him, don't you?" Dad said.

Her jaw damn near hit the floor.

"He hurt you," Dad added. "Last time."

As with most things, she'd never really talked to Dad a lot about what had happened between Josh and her. As usual, their conversation about the breakup had been something like, *He decided to move back to Promise Harbor and I couldn't leave my job here, but I'm okay with it.* Or something like that. Had Dad really known how hurt she'd been?

"Actually," she said, looking down at her feet. "I think we hurt each other."

"Did he hurt you again? If he did, I'll kick his ass." Once more she could only stare in astonishment at her father. Susan reached for his hand and slid hers into it, and they moved closer together. The sight of them supporting each other, there for each other, made her heart hurt.

"No," she choked out. "He didn't do anything."

"Do you still love him?"

Her throat completely closed up then, aching so bad. Her eyes burned and she couldn't speak. She tried to blink back the tears, shaking her head. She and Dad did not talk about things like this. Pressure rose inside her, a tight squeezing pressure, forcing the air out of her lungs, and she couldn't get more in. That light-headedness returned, her heart working in painful beats that made her muscles tighten. Jeebus. She thought she might be having a heart attack.

Or maybe she was just freaking out.

Whatever, she had to get out of there. She had to get away from this madness, back to her apartment in Boston, where she could be alone.

"Devon," Dad said, his gruff voice quiet. "We don't talk about this stuff, I know."

Okay, they were on the same page there.

"But sometimes you have to," he said. Her body twitched. He glanced at Susan again, who gave him an encouraging nod, and through her haze of panic Devon recognized somehow that this wasn't easy for him either. "I almost lost Susan because I was being like you. Don't make that mistake with Josh. If you two still care about each other..." He got a little lost and cast another helpless look at Susan.

"It's okay, Devon," she said softly. "To admit that you have feelings. It's not a weakness."

Devon stared at her, then turned half away, shoving her hands into her hair. "That's not... I know that."

"Mmmhmm."

"I don't know exactly what happened between you and Josh last time," Dad said. "But he ended up back here and you stayed in Boston."

"He ended up nearly married to someone else," Devon snapped.

"Is that what the problem is?" Susan asked. "Do you think he still loves Allie?"

Her mind went around in dizzying circles, thinking back. "No," she said. "He says he doesn't. He says he never really did. Other than as a friend. And I believe him. It just..."

"Of course it bothers you that he was going to marry someone else," Susan said. "That's normal."

It wasn't supposed to bother her. She was supposed to be over him. Once more she gazed at the carpet.

"Then what's the problem?" Susan asked.

"I know what the problem is," Dad said roughly. "The problem is you want to go back to Boston. Even if it means spending the rest of your life alone and lonely, you'd rather go back there and try to live the life your mother wanted, so you can feel worthy of her love. Isn't that right, Devon?"

Her eyes went wide, her jaw went slack and her hands fell limply to her side.

"Doug," Susan murmured.

"It's true. Isn't it?" he demanded. "You couldn't wait to get away from Promise Harbor. You couldn't wait to have all those things your mother wanted. And you couldn't wait to get away from me."

Chapter Eighteen

Devon continued to gape at her father mindlessly. *That's not true! So not true!* You *wanted* me *gone!*

Her world was crumbling around her, like the walls of the house were crashing down, like the floor was heaving beneath her feet.

"I'm sorry, Devon," he continued, his voice a rasp. "I'm sorry she did that to you. But don't let that destroy your chances of love. And happiness." She watched his fingers tighten around Susan's. More pressure built inside Devon. Her skin felt tight, like she was going to burst out of it. She couldn't take any more. With a small, choked sob, she pushed past them and rushed down the hall.

She shoved into the bedroom and shut the door behind her, leaning on it. Her hands shook, her entire body quivered and her legs had the strength of seaweed. She closed her eyes, her lungs burning. She couldn't believe Dad had said those things. All those things they'd never talked about, ever. The things *he'd* never wanted to talk about.

Now safe in her room, she never wanted to leave, never wanted to face anyone again—Dad, Susan, especially Josh. But she couldn't stay there forever. With frantic hands, she started grabbing her things and shoving them into the suitcase, her heart squeezing as she picked up some of the new things she'd bought on Greenbush Island. Tears started falling when she picked up the bottle of sunscreen Josh had bought for her, and as she pushed it into her toiletry bag, memories of his hands smoothing that lotion over her hot skin made her shiver.

Jeebus, she'd cried more tears in the last week than in all the years since her mom had left. This was ridiculous. She sniffed and swiped at her cheeks as she dumped her shoes into the bag, and then she pulled the dress from the closet, the sheer layers of peach chiffon weightless in her hands, and another sob burst out of her as she pictured Josh standing there, the look on his face when he'd seen her in the dress. *"You look beautiful."*

Agony ripped right through her core and she dropped to the bed, burying her face in her hands, the dress sliding to the floor.

Josh. Oh god, Josh.

Josh didn't even remember the drive home. He wasn't sure if he'd ever been so pissed. Okay, maybe once. And that time had involved the same woman.

He slammed into his house and paused in the kitchen, his hands gripping the counter, his head bent. Jesus, why had he let her do this to him again? Why had he thought anything would be different? He was a fucking idiot.

He didn't fucking feel sorry for her. Yeah, he wanted to help her and take care of her, but that was just him. Why wouldn't she let him? Why wouldn't she open up to him? He wasn't so stupid that he didn't know she still had feelings for him too. Goddammit! Why did she have to be so stubborn? And so blind?

He crossed to the refrigerator and pulled out a beer. *Now* he wanted a beer.

He stared out the kitchen window at his backyard. He had plans for that yard. It had been overgrown with shrubs and weeds when he'd bought the place, and he'd cleaned all that up but still hadn't had a chance to plant new things. He knew what he wanted. He just hadn't had time.

He loved his house even though he knocked around in it by himself. He loved the big yard and all the things he could do with it—a vegetable garden maybe, a small pond, even with some fish in it.

But he'd give it up if Devon would take him back.

Now that was crazy talk. He'd have to give up a lot more than his house if he were to move back to Boston. His job. His family. They were the whole reason he'd come back to Promise Harbor, after all.

Except...his mom was off on some holiday trip. With Owen, for Chrissake. His sister was away on her own and, according to Mom, doing just fine. Allie'd disappeared with Gavin. The rest of the Ralston family was off doing their own thing. Everybody seemed to be fine without him.

He lowered himself onto a stool at the counter and slumped there, the cold beer held in both hands. Huh. Maybe they all didn't need him as much as he thought they did.

That was kinda depressing.

And Devon didn't need him either.

He lifted the beer and took three long gulps, then swiped the back of his hand over his mouth.

He gave that some more thought. He'd always looked after his family. He'd helped look after Allie's family too. He didn't do it for him. He did it for them... right?

He had to examine that for a few long moments, testing it out in his mind to make sure it was true. Because he hated to think that he was some kind of codependent enabler. He shook his head. Nah. He just did it because it needed to be done.

He wasn't a hero either, despite Devon's assertion. There were enough times that he'd inwardly resented some of the demands on him. Hell yeah, he'd hated giving up his job with the special operations command in Boston. He'd fucking loved that job. Greta annoyed him at times. And his mom's insistence on keeping the business when she wasn't interested in working there and helping was stressing him out.

So then, goddammit, why *couldn't* he leave Promise Harbor? Why couldn't he go back to Boston with Devon? There really was no reason.

Yeah, he loved his job here too. He loved the town and his house, and he had lots of friends here, Stone and Ethan and Jake. It would be sad to have to sell the business, but life would go on.

But something still bothered him, and he couldn't quite put his finger on it.

Loaded down with her purse, her laptop and her suitcase, Devon stumbled out of her father's house. She hadn't wanted to face him and Susan again. In fact anger still sizzled inside her at his comments. Anger and maybe a little hurt. But she wouldn't let him know that.

Dad rose to his feet from the couch in the living room when she passed by the door with her stuff.

"You're leaving," he said.

"Yes. Thanks for letting me stay. I'll keep you posted about my job hunt."

She sensed he wanted to say more, but held back. Probably because he knew she didn't want to hear it.

He approached and picked up her suitcase. "At least let me help you carry this to the car," he said gruffly.

Susan followed, her eyes sad and the corners of her mouth tight. Guilt gave Devon a little stab at how she'd rebuffed Susan. She met the other woman's eyes. With a long, slow blink, she moved toward Susan and let her envelop her in an embrace. "I'm sorry," she whispered against Susan's hair.

Susan patted her back. "It's okay. I understand. More than you know. But I'm here if you need me. And so is your father." She met Devon's eyes. "Never doubt that, even though he won't say it himself."

Devon gave a jerky nod as she drew back.

In her car, she drove past the marina and then the beach, a few people enjoying the evening sunshine while walking on the sand, and she pressed on the brake. Staring at the ocean had always been a good way for her to gather her thoughts, to sort things out and to gain a new perspective on things. So she pulled in to a parking lot across from the beach and climbed out of her car.

She kicked off her sandals and carried them as she trudged through the soft sand, her feet sinking and making every step more work. The cool sand closed around her feet. Terns scattered out of her way, and the ocean washed onto shore in rhythmic waves. The breeze tugged at her hair, and she turned her face into it and closed her eyes, inhaling the briny scent of salt and fish and seaweed.

A little tension eased out of her body, and she let out a long, slow breath, then opened her eyes. The ocean stretched out to the horizon, blue, teal, aqua and silver, glinting in the sun. She walked a little way until she'd passed the other people there and then lowered herself to sit on the sand. She tossed her sandals aside and leaned back with her hands planted in the sand behind her.

What had Josh said...the ocean being the nurturer of all life. So huge and powerful, the exact same ocean she'd gazed upon as a girl, something that never changed, a constant. Stability in a mixed-up world.

The ache in her chest intensified again at thinking of Josh.

Had he really expected her to stay here?

As the sea air brushed over her skin and the sound of the waves lulled her, she had to admit what that ache in her heart meant. She didn't want to leave him. She didn't want to lose him again. She loved him.

His words came back to her. *"You were the one who really left, weren't you?"*

She'd spent the last year and a bit feeling the victim, the one who'd been left behind, the one who'd been rejected. And on the surface that appeared to be true.

But underneath...it wasn't that simple. When she made herself dig deep and face the truth...he was right. Oh my god, he was right.

She was the one who'd left the relationship—because she'd never admitted to Josh how she'd really felt. She'd been stubborn and focused on the things she thought she wanted, and stubborn and determined not to let on how hurt she'd been by his decision to leave. Like everything else in her life. Mother abandoned her? No big deal. A father who was distant and stoic? She was fine with that. No Christmas decorations? Whatever. No family at school the day she won the math competition? That was okay.

What would have happened if she'd told Josh how devastated she was by him leaving? What if she'd been honest and told him she loved him more than anything in the world and she didn't want him to go? What if she'd begged him to stay? Would it have made a difference?

And what if she'd told Allie the truth, that day Allie had called to tell her she and Josh were dating? What if she'd said, *Allie, I still love him...please don't do that...* Would it have made a difference?

She squeezed her eyes tightly closed at the painful realization that she'd brought much of this on herself with her stupid inability to say what she was thinking, what she was feeling.

And she had to face the truth of what her father had said too.

It hurt. A lot. The reminder that her mother hadn't loved her enough to take her with her, or to ever even come back to see her. That knowledge had settled deep inside her and shaded everything she knew about herself. But she'd never questioned why she wanted to leave Promise Harbor so much. Why she wanted the kind of career she'd chosen. Why she wanted so desperately to live somewhere urban and elegant. The idea that she was trying to please the mother she didn't even know, to prove herself worthy of her love—that had to be the most pathetic thing ever. It filled her with a burning shame that she'd been so stupid.

She couldn't leave now. Stay here forever? Well, she wasn't sure about that. Maybe. But she couldn't leave with this weight pressing down on her, her father believing she couldn't get away from him fast enough, and Josh believing...the same.

She pushed forward and bent over at the pain that shafted through her core.

Josh's face flashed in her mind, the look on it when he'd thanked her for helping, when he'd told her what a relief it was to have that taken off his shoulders.

Josh, who took *everything* on those big, strong, superhero shoulders. When a superhero could admit that he needed help...that he needed anything...well, maybe she could too.

She lifted her chin and gazed out at the water again, and the breeze on her face was especially cool now because her cheeks were damp. She pressed her hands to her wet face.

The ocean was like a collection of countless tears flowing, tears of sadness, but also tears of rejuvenation and cleansing. And so she let herself cry. For the first time in her life, she didn't try to stop the tears.

She'd screwed up. Her dad had tried to talk to her. He'd tried to tell her that he of all people understood. And she'd pushed him away, like always.

And Josh had been brave enough to tell her how he felt, which to her was the bravest thing of all, and she'd pushed him away too. She tipped her head back and looked up at the sky, clear, endless blue like the ocean, infinite and unchanging and always, always there. Tears leaked from the corners of her eyes and ran into her hair, and her throat ached.

Maybe it was too late to fix things, but she had to talk to them both, Josh and her dad, before she could leave. She had to face the truth about herself. If she ended up going back to Boston, alone, to resume her job hunt, at least she'd do it knowing that she'd been strong and brave enough to do that.

She rose to her feet and brushed the sand off the back of her skirt, bent and picked up her sandals.

She drove to her dad's place first.

When she walked in, he and Susan were sitting on the couch watching television. They both looked at her.

"Are you okay, Devon?" Susan asked, sitting forward.

"I will be. I need to talk to you, Dad."

"Do you want me to leave?" Susan asked.

Devon looked at her father, who looked at Susan and then shook his head. He reached for her hand. Devon sat down on an armchair. Susan clicked off the TV with the remote.

"I just did some thinking," she said, her voice thick. "And before I leave, I have to tell you some things."

"Go ahead."

She bent her head and looked at her fingers clasped together in her lap. "I didn't leave because I wanted to get away from you, Dad. When you said that..." She swallowed. "I never knew you thought that. The truth is, I thought you wanted me gone."

Silence. Then he said, "Why would you think that?"

"Because you never..." She paused, her throat closing up. "Because you never told me you loved me."

More silence expanded around them, filling the room. "I guess I thought you knew that," he finally said in a low voice. Devon peeked up at him through her eyelashes. This was hard for him too. She had to remember that.

"I didn't know that. I'm sorry, but I didn't. Mom had left. She didn't love me. I wanted to know that someone loved me, and you never told me. You wouldn't let me talk about it, or how it felt to be left behind."

He nodded and his throat worked. "That was a mistake."

She sank her teeth into her bottom lip. "Anyway. I guess I did have some kind of crazy idea that I could make Mom proud of me, or make her love me if I had the kind of life she'd approve of. I never realized it until you said that. It...embarrasses me." God it was hard saying that.

He nodded again. "I just wanted you to have the kind of life you wanted. For yourself, not for anyone else."

"Thank you, Dad. I..." She looked up at met his eyes directly. "I love you, Dad."

"I love you too, Dev."

Tears accumulated in the corners of her eyes again but she smiled. And he gave her a tiny smile back. Susan squeezed his hand. Maybe Devon should be thanking her for helping her Dad be brave enough to open up and say that.

"What about Josh?" Dad asked. "You still leaving?"

"I'm not sure. I'm going to go talk to him too. I...made some mistakes with him too."

Dad pursed his lips. "Telling someone you're sorry and you

love them goes a long way to making things better."

Devon huffed out a laugh and dropped her head. "Oh Dad. You are so right." She rose to her feet. "I'm going to go now, but I'll come back here tonight. Even if he doesn't want...if things don't work out, I'll stay tonight at least."

"You can stay as long as you want."

"Thank you."

She felt lighter as she left Dad's house and drove to Josh's place, filled with a sense of urgency to get to him right away. His CR-V was parked outside, and when she put her car in park, she gripped the steering wheel for a moment. The resolve inside her flickered a little, but she firmed her lips and slid out of the car.

She climbed the front steps to the veranda, absently noting the paint that had been scraped way in preparation for a new coat. What color was he going to paint the house? She nibbled her bottom lip as she rang the doorbell.

When he opened the inside door, leaving the screen between them, his eyes widened, then half shut, his mouth a straight line of unhappiness. "Devon."

"Hi." She swallowed. "Can I come in?"

Chapter Nineteen

He gave a short nod and opened the screen door too, stepping back to let her in.

She gazed at him, twisting her fingers together. Emotion rose up inside her, but she didn't know how to start. "I'm sorry," she finally whispered. "I came to tell you I'm sorry."

He lifted his chin, shoving his hands into his jeans pockets, big shoulders hunched. "For what?"

"So many things." She drew in a long, slow breath of courage. "Can we talk?"

"Sure." He led the way through the house to the great room at the back. He snagged a can of beer sitting on the counter. "Uh...would you like something? Beer? I don't know if I have any wine."

"I'm okay." Once more she just wanted to throw herself into his arms and let him hold her. Instead she perched on the edge of a chair. She dropped her purse to the rug at her feet and laid her hands on her knees. "So."

He sat on the couch across from her. "What's going on, Devon?"

"I thought about what you said. About how I was really the one who left."

He nodded slowly.

"You were right. In a way. All this time, I wanted to believe that you'd left me." She paused. It felt as if her heart was skipping every other beat. "This is hard for me."

"I know." But he held her gaze steadily. "I know it is, Dev."

His warm, unwavering gaze calmed and reassured her, and her nerves settled a little. "But I have to do it. I know. So. I felt abandoned. Betrayed. Hurt." She looked down at her hands. "Okay, hurt doesn't really even describe it. When you left..." Her throat squeezed. "I wanted to die, Josh."

His eyes flickered. "You never told me that. You never even tried to fight for us."

"I know." She held his gaze. "I know. That's why I said you were right. It was me who left. I checked out because I was too afraid to fight for us. I was too afraid to tell you how important you were to me. How much I loved you. I've never been really good at that and I didn't want to seem...pathetic."

"Nobody feels sorry for you, Dev," he said roughly, breaking the eye contact to rub his eyes. "I wish you'd get over that."

"I know. I'm trying. That's why I'm here." She swallowed. "Anyway, you said that, and when I thought about it, it was true, and it hurt, and it made me mad at myself. Same with when Allie phoned to tell me you two were seeing each other." She met his eyes again. "I lied to her, Josh. I told her I was over you and it was fine. But it wasn't fine. I wasn't over you. And i-it hurt."

His lips compressed and the corners of his eyes tightened. "Jesus Christ, Dev."

"I know. I know! I-I don't know if it would have made any difference if I'd been honest. At that point, maybe."

He covered his eyes with his hand for a moment. "This isn't all your fault, Devon."

"But I have brought some of this on myself." She had to own this if she was going to move past it. "But I couldn't have said anything when Allie phoned to ask me to come to the wedding. If you two loved each other, how could I stand in the way of that? So once again I said it was fine." She stopped, her throat aching so much she couldn't squeeze the words out. She looked down again, her bottom lip trembling. "My dad said some things, too."

He made a noise, a rough sound in his throat. "What did he say?" he growled, looking like he was ready to punch someone.

"You know about my mom," she finally managed to say in a thick voice. "How she left us."

"Yeah. I know. And I understand, Dev. I know what that did to you."

She nodded, her vision beginning to blur with yet more tears. "My dad thinks that the reason I wanted to get away from Promise Harbor, the reason I wanted that whole life I had, was because I was trying to be worthy of her love. Because if that was the kind of life she wanted, that if I had it too, maybe she'd love me."

He closed his eyes, his mouth a tight line, his jaw clenched. "I thought that too."

"Really?"

"Yeah. But yet you've never tried to contact her."

"No." He had a point there. "But it wasn't conscious. I wasn't thinking that I was going to get a job and a beautiful apartment and nice clothes and then call my mom and say, hey, come see what I've done. I really don't care about her."

He tipped his head. "I'm not sure if I believe that, but whatever. If you did, it would be understandable. She's your mother."

She squinted at him. "Do you think I *should* try to contact her?"

"Hell, I don't know. Maybe. But the thing is—it might not make any difference. If she cared about you, none of that would really matter."

Her heart gave a pinch at that, but she nodded. It was true. "Yeah. You're right. I think I just need to figure out what *I* really want from my life."

"We all need to figure that out," he said wearily, shoving a hand into his hair. "I've been doing some heavy-duty thinking too."

"Oh yeah?"

"Yeah." He met her eyes again and gave her a crooked smile. "I was thinking that I really don't need to stay here in Promise Harbor."

Her eyes flew open wide. "What? Of course you do. What about your family? The business? Your job?"

"Well. My family doesn't seem to need me much so much after all." He spread his arms wide. "None of them are even around. My job—yeah, I love it. But I loved my old job too. I do like it here in Promise Harbor. And I love my house, even though it's going to take me the rest of my life to fix it up the way I want. And as for the business...I think I could sell it. My mom would just have to understand."

She moved her head slowly side to side, taking it all in. "What are you saying?"

"Maybe you should finish first," he said.

She studied his face, the square jaw, his beautiful eyes, the resolute set of his lips. "Okay." She nodded. "I love you, Josh."

That wasn't hard to say. She'd told him that before. Once they'd gotten into their relationship, she'd felt secure and loved, more than she ever had in her life. He was the only person she'd ever told that to, other than probably her parents when she was a little girl.

Which was why he waited for more. Because that apparently didn't shock him.

"I don't want to lose you again," she continued, fighting back the wave of fear. Because this was really going to suck rocks if he told her he didn't want her. But she had to take the risk. "I want to be with you. You were right about me having nothing to go back to Boston for. I have no job there. My friends there all got weird when I lost my job, so obviously they weren't really friends. Which is probably mostly my fault. I know I don't let myself get too close to many people."

His amber eyes began to blaze.

"There's no reason I can't stay here," she said. "You don't have to offer me a job, but I can find something to do. Helping my dad more, maybe."

"Come here." He spoke with quiet firmness. She blinked at him, then rose to her feet. On shaky legs she crossed the rug and took the hand he held out to her. He tugged her down onto his lap, and then she was right where she wanted to be. In his arms.

She buried her face in the side of his neck, warm and fragrant with his singular scent. His arms closing around her felt so strong and solid.

"I love you too, Devon."

Relief washed over her in a warm wave, such profound and exquisite relief. She touched her lips to his skin, and a shudder ran through him. His arms tightened. That familiar heat and ache low down in her belly blossomed and spread, as it always did when she was around Josh, especially pressed to his body with his arms around her, but now it felt even more intense, layered with complex emotions that went so deep inside her.

She shifted in his arms and tipped her face back, and he immediately claimed her mouth with his, warm and possessive. He slid his tongue into her mouth, and she touched her own tongue to it. He groaned, softly bit her lower lip, then kissed her again. His body hardened against her, heat flaring between them as the kiss went on and on, and need for him built, powerful and compelling.

Her hands moved over him, over his shoulders so big and

strong, the soft skin at the nape of his neck, his silky hair. She couldn't get close enough, melting into the solid heat and power of his body, and she moaned into his mouth. "Josh," she whispered. "Oh, Josh."

"Mmmm." His mouth burned a trail down the side of her neck and over her shoulder, pushing aside the wide strap of her tank top, and then his hand slid down to curve over her breast. Sweet heat flowed through her, and she pressed into his palm. "Devon. We can work things out. If we love each other, we can work anything out."

"Yes." She nodded with utmost faith. "Please. I want to try to work things out, Josh."

"Right now I want to take you to bed."

"Yes," she said again. "Please."

He cupped her face with his palm and kissed her mouth, then lifted her off him. Her legs wobbled a little and heat suffused her entire body as he stood too. He slid an arm around her waist, then bent and slipped the other arm beneath her knees and lifted her into the air. She smiled and wrapped her arms around his neck, and he carried her upstairs to his bedroom.

In the dim bedroom, he lowered her to her feet beside the bed. He took her face in both hands and kissed her again, a gentle kiss of such devotion, tears sprang to her eyes. She laid her palms on his chest, felt his heartbeat thudding beneath one, and gave herself up to his endless, sensual kiss.

"So beautiful," he murmured, rubbing his rough cheek against hers. "So strong and beautiful."

"Oh Josh." She melted all over again. She didn't feel strong. Except with him.

He lifted the hem of her top, and she raised her arms so he could draw it over her head. Then she reached behind her for the zipper of her skirt. When it fell to the floor, she stood before him in her pink lace bra and panties, and his eyes darkened with appreciation as they moved over her. She felt beautiful and feminine, strong and safe. His hands moved over her body, touching her everywhere, leaving trails of sparks in their wake, and his gaze followed his hands, warming her even more.

When his hands came to rest on her shoulders, he turned her body so she faced away from him. She closed her eyes as he drew her hair to one side and kissed the back of her neck, and when he opened his mouth and so gently grazed his teeth over her flesh, fire flashed through her and she made a soft sound. He flicked open the fastener of her bra and pushed the straps down over her arms, then whisked her panties down and off. Crouching behind her, he paused for a moment to kiss the small of her back. Then he patted her butt and said, "Get on the bed."

She quickly climbed on and lay down, rolling to her side to watch him as he reached behind him and yanked his T-shirt over his head. Their eyes met and held with a sizzling connection as he unzipped his jeans and shoved them down his hips along with his boxer briefs. He kicked them aside, and her gaze tracked down over his muscled chest and abs to his erection, so bold and beautiful. She swiped her tongue over her bottom lip.

"Christ, Devon," he groaned, taking the two steps he needed to reach the bed where he joined her, sliding his big, hot body against hers. He rolled her to her back and moved over her, kissing her again. She held on to him, parted her legs so he fit between them, so perfect, and kissed him back with everything she had. His weight on her was a delicious pressure.

She still wasn't sure what was happening with them, between them. This time it seemed like they were both willing to give things up, but that had to be easier to work out than neither of them willing to concede. More and more, she found herself wanting to stay in Promise Harbor, wanting to fix things between her and her dad, wanting to see how things worked out between him and Susan, wanting to help Josh keep the family business going and maybe wanting to help her dad too.

But really she just wanted to be with Josh.

"I love you," she whispered as he moved his mouth from hers.

"Love you too, baby." He kissed his way down her neck, then her chest, then he closed his mouth over the nipple of one breast and tugged at it. Pleasure streamed straight to her womb, and she arched into his mouth with a soft cry. He closed his hand over her other breast in a gentle squeeze. "Mmm."

Her eyes fell closed and she gave herself over to his touch. With his hands and his mouth, he drew a veil of magic and warmth and love around them, shrouding them both in heat and light and love. And the words fell from her lips, so easily. "I love you, I love you."

He moved his mouth to her other breast, caught the wet nipple between his fingers and pulled, and the sensation on both nipples had her body twitching hard beneath him. Her hips lifted into his, aching with need for him. "Please," she murmured, sliding her hands into his hair. "Please, Josh. Need you."

"Say it again." He lifted his head, and she opened her eyes to see his gaze fixed on her intently.

"I need you." It felt so good, so liberating and giving, she said it again. "I need you, Josh, so much."

His eyes warmed and his lips curved into a sexy smile. "Good girl."

She should have been annoyed at that, but instead his words pleased her and she smiled too. She rubbed his silky hair between her fingers. "Need you inside me."

His smile deepened. "Yeah."

He moved up on her, his knees pushing her thighs wide, and she watched as he fisted his cock. He hesitated and met her eyes again. "Okay with no condom?"

She bit her lip briefly. "I'm okay. You okay?"

He nodded. "Yeah."

He didn't need to say more. They understood each other, understood that this was about trust and intimacy and deepening their relationship, and she loved him so much for asking.

When he pushed into her, it felt incredibly good. He moved so deep inside her, he touched nerve endings that thrilled her and filled her with such aching pleasure, so deep he touched her heart, touched her soul. She watched his face, entranced, as his eyes fell closed, his long eyelashes resting on his cheeks, and then he fell over her, taking his weight on his elbows, his arms sliding around her head, one hand coming on to her forehead in a possessive, protective gesture that softened her heart and made her go liquid around him.

Her body closed around him, pulling him in, and she wrapped her arms around his back and her legs around his waist as he moved against her. Their bodies pushed together, seeking more, finding a rhythm that matched the beating of their hearts. His breath rushed hot over the skin of her neck. "Devon, god Devon, don't leave me."

"I won't. I never will."

Sensation spiraled inside her, a taut coil of pleasure and heat, everything inside her tightening, pulling hard, up and up.

"Yes," she urged him. "Yes, yes...oh god."

He rose up again onto his knees, spread wide between her thighs. He cupped her breasts, thumbed her nipples, then slid his hands down her rib cage to close around her waist, holding her as he thrust harder into her. Once more their eyes met, his blazing at her with a golden flame, full of worship and devotion.

She felt so lucky, grateful to have this man, this superhero, in her life, loving her, and she wanted to give him so much—anything. Everything.

She loved him.

More than the love she'd felt for him before, this time it felt stronger, as mighty and bottomless and immeasurable as the ocean—because nothing stood between them now. Everything was out there. Because she'd taken the risk, shared parts of herself with him she never had before. Because she'd given him her whole self this time, all her flaws and insecurities and fears. And he loved her anyway.

Emotion swelled and rushed through her. He reached for her hands and held them, and she tightened her fingers around his, still holding his gaze. She never wanted to let him go, never wanted him to let her go, and she gripped his hands as her climax burst upon her, an explosion of sparks and heat, pleasure sliding outward from her core, lovely and warm and sweet.

"Love you," she gasped. "Oh god, I love you." With their clasped hands at her chest, his eyes fell closed, and his body tensed and went still for long, pulsing moments, and then once again he stretched out over her.

"Love you too," he groaned against her neck. "I love you too."

"I know I don't have to offer you a job," Josh said a long time later. They still lay in bed, wrapped up in sheets and each other's arms, lounging in somnolent satisfaction. He ran his hand down the silky curve of her back. "And I do know that's not the kind of work you've always wanted to do. But you really are helping me, Dev. Doing stuff I have no clue about." He slid his hand up and into her hair and tugged until she looked up at him. "I need you, Dev. But not just for that. That was a huge load off my mind, but I need you for so much more."

"I need you too," she whispered. "And it scares the crap out of me. But if my dad can admit he has feelings for someone...whoa. And if you—a superhero—can say it, I can too."

His lips quirked. "I kinda like how you think I'm a superhero."

She smiled and rubbed her body enticingly against his. "When you left, I kept telling myself I'd find someone else. Someone like you. Someone who's loyal to his family and honorable and responsible. It was kind of funny, because the things I loved the most about you were the things that took you away from me."

"I'm sorry too, Dev. It wasn't all your fault. We both could have done things differently."

"If I'd begged you to stay in Boston with me, would you have?" She tipped her head.

He thought about it. "Honestly? I'm not sure. I was pretty terrified about my mom and everything that was happening when Allie's mom died. But I do know...I really *wanted* you to beg me to stay."

"I should have told you," she said in a choked voice. "I thought telling you how much I wanted you to stay made me seem weak and pathetic. Like when my mom left and I begged her not to go without me."

"Fuck." He drew her closer and pressed his face to her hair. "I should have realized. I should have known how hard that was for you."

She *hadn't* been fine with him and Allie seeing each other or getting married. Of course she hadn't. He couldn't speak for Allie of course, but had they been willing to accept Devon's words at face value to ease their own consciences?

And maybe he'd been willing to accept her words at face value because he needed to believe that *he* was the one who'd been wronged when he left Boston to move back to Promise Harbor. Because if Devon had really loved him, she would have come with him. Wasn't that what he'd always believed? So she *couldn't* be hurt by him and Allie being together, because she'd made her choice to stay when she knew he had to leave.

So, Allie'd done her duty by calling Devon, making sure she was okay with it all, and then they'd forgotten all about her so they could just move on with things, with making everyone else happy by getting married. He wanted to roar with anger and pain now, feeling like a hot knife was twisting in his heart. But he forced himself to breathe, to relax, to not squeeze Devon so tight he might pop her eyeballs out of her head, even though he wanted to.

"No." Her head moved against him. "It wasn't your fault. I just have this weird hang-up. I'm working on it. But it wasn't just that, Josh. I knew what you were like—I knew how important it was to look after your family. How could I have stood in the way of what you had to do?"

"Oh my god, Dev." He closed his eyes, his throat tight, emotion surging up from his chest. And there was the thing that had been bothering him. Because he'd been so focused on how she should have been willing to open herself up to him, he hadn't even realized that, in a way, she'd been making a sacrifice for him. Overwhelming gratitude and love for her washed over him like an ocean breaker, and he held on to her tighter for long moments.

"What about Allie?" Devon whispered eventually.

"I thought we already talked about that. Allie and I are done."

"It's going to make things weird between your families, isn't it?"

"Maybe."

"I was kind of afraid about that. That you'd put that first, instead of us."

They moved so their eyes met, and he touched her chin. "No," he said firmly. "You come first with me, Devon. I want you to know that, without a doubt. Whatever happens, know that."

She nodded, her lower lip quivering, her eyes full of love and trust that made him feel—fuck yeah—like a superhero.

"When—if—Allie comes back, we'll figure things out. But now it's you and me, Dev." He paused. "I wish you and Allie could be friends again."

"Yeah," she whispered. "I do too. I miss her. But I don't know…"

"Can you forgive her?"

Her lips quirked. "Yeah. I think I can. Since you're *mine* now."

He grinned. "Okay, so how about we stay here for now, since you have no reason to rush back to Boston. You help with the business, maybe help out your dad too. Get to know Promise Harbor again. Help me decorate my house. And we'll see how things go, and if you want to move back to Boston, we'll talk about that."

"Yes," she said. "I do want to stay here with you. I'll try to be better. I want to be a superhero like you." He chuckled and pressed her head into his chest again. And she said just what he was feeling too… "I want to be worthy of someone like you."

About the Author

Kelly Jamieson lives in Winnipeg, Canada and is the bestselling author of over twenty romance novels and novellas. Her writing has been described as "emotionally complex", "sweet and satisfying" and "blisteringly sexy". If she can stop herself from reading or writing, she loves to cook. She has shelves of cookbooks that she reads at length. She also enjoys gardening in the summer, and in the winter she likes to read gardening magazines and seed catalogues (there might be a theme here...). She also loves shopping, especially for clothes and shoes. She loves hearing from readers, so please visit her website at www.kellyjamieson.com or contact her at info@kellyjamieson.com.

You're invited to the wedding of the year

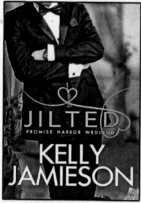

JILTED
PROMISE HARBOR WEDDING
KELLY JAMIESON

Book 1

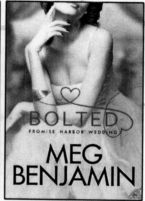

BOLTED
PROMISE HARBOR WEDDING
MEG BENJAMIN

Book 2

BUSTED
PROMISE HARBOR WEDDING
SYDNEY SOMERS

Book 3

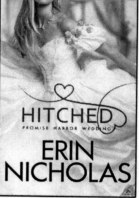

HITCHED
PROMISE HARBOR WEDDING
ERIN NICHOLAS

Book 4

Don't miss any of the books in the Promise Harbor Wedding series

It's all about the story...

Romance

HORROR

www.samhainpublishing.com

CPSIA information can be obtained at www.ICGtesting.com
Printed in the USA
LVOW08s1104201213

366212LV00003B/303/P